The Silver Locket

Marie Fostino

SPECIAL EDITION

Andrea Ford Books
CREATIVE FLIGHT PUBLISHING
Newark

Copyright © Marie Fostino – September 2011

All rights reserved. Except as permitted under the U.S. Copyright Act of 1976, no part of this publication may be reproduced, distributed, or transmitted in any form or by any means, or stored in a database or retrieval system, without prior written permission from the publisher.

Creative Flight Publishing

Visit our website at www.creativeflightpub.com

Creative Flight Publishing is a sole proprietorship under the control of Andrea Lynn Ford.

The characters and events portrayed in this book are fictitious. Any similarity to real persons, living or dead, is coincidental and not intended by the author.

ISBN-13: 978-0989003315

Printed in the United States of America

☦
SPECIAL EDITION

Acknowledgements

We all were once young and in love. We have all made mistakes and hopefully we have learned from them and passed this knowledge down to our little ones. This book came from my heart to show that there is still good in the world. With God's love, and the love for each other, we can withstand the trials and tribulations that life throws at us. Nothing is too big for us to carry with the support and help of family.

This book is dedicated to my husband, five children, and my seven grandchildren. Thank you for the love that we share during our adventure of life, and for your patience as I wrote this book.

I also want to thank all of the wonderful individuals who contributed in the making of this book.

Last, but not least, I would like to thank you, the reader, for taking the time to read what I have written. I hope you enjoy this book.

Praise for The Silver Locket

"Life defined - The trials and tribulation of teaching, loving, caring, protecting, nurturing, defending, and guiding to name a few...The Silver Locket teaches all of these aspects of life and then some." *Amazon Review, 4 Stars*

"This is a book written straight from every parent's heart. We all struggle with how to talk to our children about morality in a day where the world says anything goes and balance this with how much we still love our children even when their feet stumble. The author tells the story with the wisdom of a parent that knows that with God, nothing is ever wasted in our lives."
Amazon Review, 5 Stars

"If you are a teenager or a parent with a teenager, this is a must read! I have a 12 year old that LOVED the book and it really opened her eyes to what it would be like to be a pregnant kid in high school." *Amazon Review, 5 Stars*

"If you are looking for a quick, intriguing, light romance novel then look no further. The Silver Locket by Marie Fostino is truly moving and inspired by a true story."
Teen Diaries Online Magazine, 5 Stars

"The Silver Locket is a beautiful, heartwarming coming of age story of first love, loss, teenage pregnancy and the strength of family." *Bottles and Book Reviews, 5 Stars*

"Marie's story is one that just about anyone between the ages of 14 and 75 could relate to. A well written story of a young lady and a young man trying to find their way, making mistakes that can't be undone, but with the help and support of a Godly family, lessons are learned and tragedy is overcome by love. I would recommend this book very highly and will be gifting this book to all of my daughter-in-laws and hopefully they will pass it on to their children as they are old enough."
Barnes & Noble Review, 4 Stars

"There are many things that can be discussed after reading this book, which is written in a way that both young adults and parents can appreciate. The descriptions and dialogue are believable and this book is a very quick read—and trust me when I say that. I'm the slowest reader I know."
Goodreads Review, 4 Stars

"Put simply, this book was amazing."
Skelations Online Review

Contents

Prologue		1
1.	The Present Day	3
2.	Flashback	11
3.	New School – New Friends	17
4.	Ignoring The Red Flags	21
5.	Family Night	27
6.	Jacy's Bold Move	33
7.	The Apology	37
8.	A Different Family Night	43
9.	True Friends?	49
10.	A Family Thanksgiving	56
11.	Sixteen And Confused	63
12.	The Rave Party	71
13.	Sneaking Out	78
14.	The Final Temptation	84
15.	The Scare	95
16.	Jail Time	105
17.	The Best Laid Plans	112
18.	Sharing The News	121
19.	Crash Course In Motherhood	127
20.	A Difficult Decision	135
21.	The Big News	145
22.	The Holidays	150

23. Fearing The Worst	160
24. A Baby Too Soon?	167
25. Life & Death	173
26. Facing Reality	181
27. Reality Sets In	188
28. Life Goes On	196
29. Back To Present	202

Prologue

People often stopped Jenny on the street to ask if the child by her side was her younger sister, but she was not embarrassed to say, "No, this is my child." Yet some of the looks she drew from others certainly bothered her.

Jenny had to seriously think about her past and her future. She was 16 years old when her life changed forever. Despite being raised in a Christian home with strict religious values, some of her choices were careless... and they came with weighty consequences.

Today as the mother of a teenage daughter, she views the world with the eyes of an adult. She looks back and clearly sees how different she viewed life back then - so childishly irresponsible. Her family stood behind her during those difficult times but she did not truly appreciate their support. Recalling her rebellious years, she hopes Janie will not follow in her footsteps.

A strange combination of sadness and joy overcome her when she turns back the clock. Names and faces float through her mind like ghosts that still haunted her, but as always, a smile forms on her face and she remembers only love.

This may seem like a typical teenage story, as you read

of her getting into trouble like most teenagers do - you will smile, you might even get mad, and at some points you might also cry. However, her name is Jenny Federigo, and this is her story. Don't say you haven't been warned.

1. The Present Day

Jenny fervently pushed down on the gas pedal. It was 3:25 in the afternoon and she was anxious to get home. As she drove her green Camaro on a warm windy day, tiredness consumed her. She had run all day at work, talking to customers and writing receipts. She worked for the city helping people acquire permission for legal additions to properties – not the most difficult job but she was also a single mom, with plenty of chores to do when she got home. However, she still needed to go shopping for the party, and fought off the exhaustion.

Jenny glanced into the overhead mirror. The image staring back at her reflected her mother's rich Italian features as well as her father's distinctly Indian traits. Her skin was a beautiful olive color, her hair long and dark, and her eyes a deep brown.

Her daughter Janie, usually went to her grandmother Marie's house after school. She had promised her that after school that day they would go to the mall. Entering her mother's driveway with the windows rolled down, she could hear the wind ringing through the chimes on the front porch. As she strode up the sidewalk to the front steps many memories of growing up in that two-story house embraced her. The screen door was open so she let herself in and it slammed behind her.

"Janie?" her mother called. "Is that you?"

Marie thought it might be her granddaughter arriving home from school. She had just taken chocolate chip cookies out of the oven and hoped to surprise her.

When Jenny entered the kitchen she sucked in a big whiff. It was a familiar smell that she remembered from childhood. She shut her eyes for a moment to reminisce. As her mom placed the cookies on a cooling rack, Jenny walked over and planted a soft kiss on her cheek. It felt good to be home in familiar surroundings.

"Isn't Janie home yet?" Jenny asked.

"No," Marie replied, brushing a few grey hairs from her temples.

Marie had been busy in the kitchen for hours, and the warmth of the day along with the heat of the oven left her feeling somewhat bedraggled. Even so, the 50-year-old still looked younger than her years with only a few lines around her eyes. She had also baked a cake because another one of her grandchildren was celebrating her first birthday. Raising a spatula, Marie scooped some white frosting out of a bowl and spooned it onto the cake. Jenny grabbed a hot cookie, tossed the treat hand to hand and blew on it to cool it down before taking a bite. Then she went to the fridge for a glass of cold milk - the perfect drink in which to dip the cookie. This was a habit she had acquired and loved while growing up.

As always, Jenny glanced at two framed pictures on the wall leading from the kitchen to the living room. One contained a newspaper article about the bridge that was finally built over a set of railroad tracks near the local high school. Jenny had pushed for that bridge, and was proud of that accomplishment. She had quite a struggle getting the town to accept the idea. She gathered countless signatures so the city would create a traffic statement to determine if a bridge was really necessary. The other frame displayed a train smashed into a pickup truck – a devastating accident that added fire to her determination and still pulled painfully at her heart. She finished her cookie, put two fingers to her lips, kissed them and gently let them touch the picture.

Entering the living room, Jenny stared out the front window. Then she turned and scanned the room. It had undergone a complete metamorphosis over the years. When she was young the couch was a swirl of pastel pink and blue in a unique design. In front of it sat a big blue throw rug with a pink and blue border. The television was an old-fashion console model with pictures of five small children sitting on top. She now saw a color scheme of brown and beige with light beige carpeting - one thing her parents would not have when she and her siblings were young. There was also a modern plasma TV. The picture window, which used to be covered in drapes tied at each side, now, had only shades. She marveled at how so many things had changed over the years, yet so many other things remained exactly the same. An odd mixture of past and present melded together into the present day.

Jenny began to pace the living room. *Where is Janie?* She wondered.

Marie entered and immediately sensed her daughter's concern.

"Settle down," she said. "She should be here any moment."

Marie gently squeezed her daughter's shoulder. As a mother herself for thirty years, she knew full well what it was like to worry about one's child. Jenny's body tensed as she leaned by the front door peering out a small side window. Her angst was evidenced by her crossed ankles and tightly wrapped arms around her waist.

"She should have been home already, mom."

Although Jenny tried to remain calm, fear overcame her and once again she paced the room. *Why is she so late?* Her imagination ran wild with thoughts of Janie doing something she knew she shouldn't. Remembering her own teen years, she feared that her daughter might be involved with the wrong crowd – hanging around after school smoking and taking drugs. She hated the way her mind conjured up such dreadful images. *Why can't I just be positive instead of envisioning such awful things?*

§

Janie was on her way home but became sidetracked when two boys grabbed her trumpet case and backpack. She raced after them forcing her legs to run faster without letting them trip her up. She should have turned right at the corner but they ran to the left, which left her no choice but to go the wrong way to catch up with them.

"Come on," huffed Janie with a lighthearted giggle. "Please stop!" The wind howled down Martin Street making it difficult to run.

"Ha, ha," Carl laughed as he ran.

Whenever she got close, he turned inadvertently. For a second she thought she caught him, but he swiftly jogged to the right catching her off guard. Then she fell, twisted her ankle, and landed on her knees. She knew she would be in trouble when her mother saw the grass stains on her pants. *She always thinks the worst*, Janie thought.

"Oh, Janie," Jose sang playfully, "I have something that belongs to you."

They ran off the sidewalk and veered onto a green

pathway where a couple of dogs ran with their owners and some kids played catch. She ran in between them trying to grab her belongings sometimes closing in, yet they always managed to get away.

§

Marie put her arms around Jenny and offered a gentle hug.

"I'm sure she's fine," she said in a comforting tone. "She's a good girl. Remember when you were 14?"

"Yeah, I remember," she replied. "That's why I'm so worried."

Jenny automatically touched the silver heart locket around her neck. Even though she felt a sense of accomplishment for being able to care well for her daughter, she wanted more for her. She definitely did not want her to make the same mistakes she made at that age.

Marie recalled her daughter's difficulties and winced. She would do anything to wipe away Jenny's memory of those times, but knew that those unexpected and difficult problems helped mold her into the kind of woman she was today.

"Let's go back to the kitchen," she suggested. "You can help me frost with the cake. I'm sure Janie will be here soon."

Marie took her daughter's hand and coaxed her to follow. Just then the door swung open and Janie ran in laughing. As she entered, the door slammed against the wall prompting her to yell, "Sorry!"

She was thirty minutes late. Not only was she huffing and puffing but also her hair straggled around her face and her braid was a mess. Her knees were covered with grass stains and her shirt stuck out of her pants. She stood for a moment in the hallway and took in the scent of fresh-baked cookies. She could not resist. Completely forgetting about the mall, she headed for the kitchen.

"Mm... cookies," she squealed running past her mother and grandmother.

"Stop right there, young lady!" Jenny hollered wagging a finger. "Where on earth have you been? And look at you! What in heaven's name have you been doing?"

Marie turned and left the room to give mother and daughter some privacy.

"You know you're supposed to be home right after school," Jenny added leaning over Janie's slender form. Her body stiffened and her hands clutched into fists at her side. She wanted answers – and fast before her awful thoughts made her even more upset. Janie hung her head as she listened to her mother.

"You were only ten minutes from here," she said. "You know you're not allowed to stop and talk or visit with anyone."

Janie shot her head up and glared at her mother the second she stopped talking. *What did I do wrong?* She wondered as she focused on her mother's questioning eyes.

Janie tossed down her backpack and instrument case, crossed her arms, spread her legs and stood rigidly – defiantly so - in front of her mother. She was tired of all the lectures. *Why can't she just let me have a little fun now and then?*

"I'm not like you, mom," she said finally, her face flushed with anger. "You taught me right from wrong and I didn't do anything bad."

Janie was just beginning to notice boys but even though teenage hormones were coming into play, she still acted more like a child. She did not care about makeup or what she looked like. Even so, she figured a few of the boys liked her anyway. Heck, they would not pull her braid or take her things to make her chase them if they didn't. She had to admit that she enjoyed the attention; it was just innocent fun.

Tears formed in Janie's eyes because she knew what her mother thought. She hated being accused of something before they even talked. *How dare she think that way*, Janie thought indignantly. I'm a kid and I have friends. *Why doesn't she trust me?*

She paused to take a breath and recalled her mother's lectures on not following the crowd or taking drugs. She already knew about sex because mom was honest and open about life.

"I'm not going to make the same mistakes you did," she blurted out, and immediately wished she hadn't.

The ensuing silence was deafening as mother and daughter glared at each other. Jenny focused on her daughter's eyes and could see Jacy all over again. Sometimes it hurt to see him in her, but she did not want to forget the times they shared together.

They stared at each other for a long moment. Then Janie sighed aloud, turned and headed for the stairs. She deliberately pounded her feet on each step and when she reached her room, she slammed the door forcefully. Marie heard the noise and joined her daughter in the living room.

"Don't you think you're being a little too hard on her," she suggested wiping her hands with a towel.

She could see the pain in her daughter's eyes and felt helpless. She knew Jenny had only good intentions for Janie but she also realized that even the best of intentions could lead one to overreact. Jenny began to cry and turned toward the front door. Again despite her better judgment, she had considered the worst.

"I've got to get some air," she said. Jenny pulled her car keys from her purse, and hurried out the front door.

2. Flashback

Jenny was raised in Fort Wayne, Indiana. In that corner of the world, the Federigo family enjoyed all four seasons: spring as it blossomed with fresh new life, the sweltering heat of the summer, fall with its amazingly colored leaves, and the chilly snows of winter. Her doting parents, Jim and Marie, offered a loving and protective environment to their children. Jenny's carefree life was filled with softball games and soccer teams, as well as bike riding like most families in the area. One of her favorite places to go was the local children's zoo with its skyline and train ride. They usually stopped to see the giraffes, lions, and kangaroos, but she really loved the petting zoo where she could help give bottles to the baby animals.

Fort Wayne was referred to as the City Of Churches, a nickname that stretched back to the late 1800's when the city was a hub for regional Catholic, Lutheran and Episcopal faiths. Jenny's family attended a Fundamental Baptist Church where they sang in the choir and volunteered their time with fundraisers. Jenny volunteered once a month by helping in the nursery where she loved caring for the babies during the church service. The youngest ones sometimes became frightened, but she sang to them in their bassinets to calm them down. Once they reached about six months, she held them, rocked them or fed them their bottles. Thus her maternal instincts developed when she was still a teenager.

Jenny's best friend and reading buddy was Ashley - a slightly overweight girl with red hair and pale skin. They became friends as young children, and continued to remain close into their teen years. They both preferred to keep their noses in books instead of hanging out with the kids at school. Who needed other friends when you had a reading partner?

Jenny took part in sports, but only because her mother insisted. She much preferred delving into a good book, while her siblings watched television. She particularly loved the series Sweet Valley High and The Secret Garden. At school, she was a good student who kept up her grades much to the delight of her teachers. She liked school, especially chatting in the halls with Ashley whenever the opportunity arose. She enjoyed her first year of high school as a freshman and looked forward to the next three years. Little did she know, this was not meant to be.

§

During the summer before Grade 10 began, Jenny's father came home with startling news. Jim was offered a promotion and increased salary to take a job out of state. He managed a large baking company that planned to open a new plant about an hour outside of Oklahoma City. The family would have to move so he could start up the plant, and Marie would need to quit her job at the beauty shop. After discussing the pros and cons of such a move, Jim and Marie came to the conclusion that the kids were still young and could adjust. They figured that their eldest daughter, Kristina, would likely be the most distressed since she was a senior in high school, but agreed that the move would further Jim's career, and prove to be beneficial overall to the family.

A family meeting was held amid much protest, moaning, and groaning from the children. As they expected, Kristina complained about leaving her friends, and graduating with a bunch of new acquaintances instead of all of those who were already dear to her. However, her parents reminded her that in just one more year she'd be leaving to attend college anyway, and she might just as well learn to make new friends. That did not go over well. At the other end of the spectrum, Jenny's brother Erik was excited about this new adventure while Jenny's younger sisters, Jessica and Regina, were too young to care.

Since her parents had already made up their minds, the plan was put into motion. By the end of summer, Jim had secured appropriate housing, their Indiana house was packed up and the movers picked up their belongings. Jenny cried when she said goodbye to Ashley, but promised to write. She did not have many close friends at school, and really did not care, but she and Ashley were like peanut butter and jelly – they just fit together and were linked at the hips like sisters. They knew each other so well and the thought of leaving her best friend broke her heart.

Jim drove his 1994 GMC Safari with Erik and Kristina in his car. The drive was long with bathroom and snack stops along the way. Erik wore his headphones with Metallica blasting in his ears, while Kristina read books. Although uncomfortable about driving so far, Marie followed him in her 1994 Pontiac Grand Am with Jenny and the little ones. Jessica and Regina played games in the back seat along the way and every few miles asked, "Are we there yet?"

As the sun began to set, Jim stopped at a hotel because

he knew Marie feared driving at night. The children were happy to stop because Jenny's parents made the trip an adventure. They enjoyed swimming in the hotel's pool and going out for dinner. After a good night's sleep, the morning sun reminded them to get back on the road. By the time the next evening arrived, the family reached their new home. However, they could not stay there because the movers were not due until the following day so it was off to another hotel for the night.

When they went back to the two-story house, the movers had arrived. The house had five bedrooms, which meant Jessica and Regina would share a room. Marie let the kids take part in decorating their rooms, picking out the bedspreads and sheets, and letting them choose the colors of paint for the walls. Disgruntled, Jenny could not help noticing the lack of greenery in the area. The landscape was entirely different with flat plains stretching as far as the eye could see.

§

It was a warm and windy day when school began that fall. All the children would be the new kids on the block. They had never experienced this before, and each took it differently. Kristina decided that keeping her grades up was more important than making friends. Her new school did not accept the same credits as the last one, so she took it upon herself to take extra classes and study. Erik and the youngest girls did not seem to mind their new school. As for Jenny, she definitely did not like being a sophomore with students she did not know. After just a month, she had had enough.

"Mom," she groaned, "why did we have to move

here?"

"You know why, honey," said Marie. "Your dad got a new job." She opened the fridge to see what she could make for dinner.

"I hate it here," Jenny replied sullenly.

She was quite unhappy and wanted her mother to know it. Marie glanced up at her daughter. She looked so down in the dumps and Marie could not help feeling badly for her. However, she also knew that sometimes it was necessary to make sacrifices in life. Although it was difficult to uproot the entire brood, Jim obtained a position that would help the family out more than before.

"Honey, you haven't given it enough time," Marie noted. She grabbed frozen vegetables and chicken from the freezer just as Jessica and Regina ran into the kitchen.

"Dinner ready yet?" They chimed in unison.

Marie caught and kissed both of them on the forehead. In response, they squeezed her tightly around the waist.

"Not yet. Did you do your homework?"

"Awe," they moaned retreating back to the living room.

"And turn off the TV," she shouted behind them. Marie stirred the pot of vegetables and turned toward Jenny.

"Haven't you made any friends yet?"

"No," Jenny replied stubbornly. "No one wants to be friends with someone who is new and not a freshman. No one even talks to me," she added slumping into a kitchen chair. She crossed her arms on the table and let her head rest on her arms. "I miss Ashley," she muffled.

Marie drew near, played with Jenny's hair and gently caressed her head. She knew her job was to encourage her daughter and get her motivated to make friends - not an easy task.

"Honey, sometimes you have to be a friend, before you can make a friend," she soothed, but Jenny did not respond. "Give it some more time. By the way," she smiled, "I got a job at a beauty shop here in town."

"Great. Someone even likes you already," she whined and rolled her eyes. *It's just not fair*, Jenny thought. *How am I supposed to find another Ashley?*

"Come and help me set the table," Marie suggested. "Tomorrow will be another day."

3. New School - New Friends

The following day, Jenny was far from thrilled with the prospect of trying to make new friends but to her surprise someone did talk to her.

"Hey," she heard as she sauntered along the hallway.

A petite pretty young girl dressed entirely in black with dark lipstick and a gold chain around her waist stood in front of her. Jenny had seen her in the halls before but did not really take notice. And she was not the kind of girl her parents would like her to know. However, no one else had befriended her yet so she was happy that someone approached her.

"I'm Sandy," the girl announced. "Do you have a smoke?"

Jenny's eyes grew as big as saucers. The last bell rang and lockers slammed shut while other students pushed and shoved their way down the hall to get out the school doors. Jenny dropped one of her books and stooped down to get it. Then she looked up at Sandy and shook her head.

"No, I don't smoke," she said softly.

"New around here?" Sandy asked sincerely.

"Yeah."

"Then come and meet the gang?"

A red flag flew up in Jenny's mind and she hesitated for a moment but then chose to ignore it. No one else seemed interested in her and just the fact that Sandy said hello made her feel better. Letting her guard down, she followed Sandy across the street to a spot where a group of teenagers stood smoking and chatting. They looked like they were having a good time.

"Anyone got a smoke?" Sandy yelled.

Jenny stood awkwardly next to her and let her eyes scan the ground.

"Here," said one of the boys throwing her a cigarette. "Need a light?"

Sandy inhaled slowly before letting the smoke escape through her nose. "This is Jenny," she announced between coughs.

As Sandy introduced her to each of them, she glanced up shyly. First there was Susan, medium height and skinny with short red hair that waved around her face. She wore thick black eye makeup and lipstick, with long dangling earrings. Then there was Amanda, a tall and lean girl about a year older than the rest with long dirty blonde hair. Her skirt was so short that if she bent over, her behind would show. Amanda did not have enough credits to progress to the eleventh grade so she was a year behind. However, she did have a car and a driver's license. Gary was lanky with a shaved head except on the top where there was some black spiked hair. Jenny noticed his tight jeans and cute smile. Last but not least was Jacy, a tall muscular Native Indian with long black hair pulled into a ponytail, dark brown eyes and an irresistible smile.

"Hi," said Jacy, his eyes twinkling. He held out his pack of smokes and shook it until a cigarette popped up. Then he offered it to her.

"No thanks," Jenny replied. *What am I doing here?* She thought.

Jacy took the smoke out and lit it. "So you're new

around here?" He asked, the cigarette hanging from his mouth.

Jenny suddenly felt flushed and her hands became sweaty. As the teens continued to talk, the sun played between the clouds making shadows on their faces. The wind was warm, offering the only comfortable feeling at the time. She recalled how she avoided kids like this when she hung around with Ashley. The warning signs told her to run but her legs did not respond.

"Where did you move from?" Jacy asked.

"Indiana."

"You a freshman?"

"No."

"Sucks being you."

"Tell me about it."

"Where do you live?"

"Menard Street and 108th," she whispered, her head still down and kicking a stone.

Jacy's eyes widened and a huge smile formed on his face. He took another drag of his cigarette letting the smoke slowly stream from his mouth.

"That's where I live," he laughed.

Jenny's eyes flashed up at him and noticed that he was looking past her. She turned and followed his gaze.

"Got the feeling you missed the bus," he said.

Jenny let out a long sigh. The walk home would be a long one.

"Got to go," she said shrugging her shoulders.

Jenny stared at the ground ahead as she walked away. She knew her mother would grill her with questions by the time she got home so she picked up her pace. Then she heard Jacy call out her name.

"Come on," he said attempting to catch up to her.

"You're on my way. Want a ride?"

"Who's driving?" Jenny asked.

"Amanda. She always drives me home. We got room," he added, his eyes beckoning.

Jenny paused for a moment. She was not allowed in a car with a teenager. Not yet anyway.

"Your call," Jacy said with a grin.

He took the last drag of his smoke before throwing the butt on the ground. Then he turned around and followed the rest of the group to the parking lot. Jenny felt conflicted. She could hear her mother telling her that accidents happened because kids often act so irresponsibly in cars. They did not understand how important it was to leave the driver alone, not blast the radio and wear their seatbelts. Then she thought of the long walk ahead of her.

"Wait for me!" She yelled.

4. Ignoring The Red Flags

The next morning on the way to school, Jenny slouched on the seat of the bus.

Why did dad have to change jobs, she questioned in her mind. Life was great in Indiana. I miss Ashley so much.

She used to spend countless hours talking and reading with her. They loved eating pizza and comparing the adventures within the pages of their books. Right then and there, she decided that when she was a mother, she would not move her children around and make their lives miserable.

Most of the seats on the bus were taken when three boys, including Jacy got on so they dropped into the seats next to her. He conversed with his friends and did not look at her. Jenny gazed out the window, her mind jumping to another time and place where she enjoyed the company of her old friend. When the bus arrived at the school, she was forced to squeeze and shove her way off. As she made her way along the crowed school halls, she did not feel much better. It seemed as if she was physically pushed from one class to the next.

The morning passed slowly as she listened with little interest to her teachers. The Oklahoma school system seemed somewhat behind that of Indiana so it was more like a review on each subject. Finally, the bell rang for lunch. The school had an open campus, which meant the students could eat in the cafeteria or leave the school grounds as long as they were back in time for their next class. Since a McDonald's was just down the street, Jenny decided to go there.

When she walked out of the building, the schoolyard was packed with teenagers. She could hear kids gossiping in little clicks here and there. Some sat opening their lunch bags, enjoying the sunshine. Others stood around looking at people and talking about them. A police officer walked around the school property to ensure that no one was smoking. The teens that did smoke stood across the street.

A guard at the crosswalk made sure the students crossed the street safely. While Jenny waited to cross, she heard her name called.

"Hey," said a familiar voice.

Quickly she turned and noticed the tall Indian fellow staring at her. Sandy, Susan and Amanda stood in a huddle talking and turned around when Jacy spoke. They waved when she flashed her eyes up at them and she waved back.

"How's it going?" Jacy asked as he reached her. He took out his pack of smokes and offered her one.

"No thanks. I told you I don't smoke."

Jacy shrugged his shoulders nonchalantly, smiled and slid the pack back into his pocket.

Jenny decided that this time she was not going to get into trouble. She would have lunch and nothing would get in her way. She turned away from Jacy and headed for the McDonald's but it was not long before she realized that he was following her.

"Where you going?" He asked trying to keep up with her pace.

"Mickey D's."

"Want some company?"

"Sure, why not?"

She continued her quick pace with just another block to go. When they entered McDonald's, some kids pushed past them to get in line first. They also had to dodge ketchup packs and wadded up napkins thrown by the new freshman. At the counter four people were taking orders and the line was long. Lunch lasted only an hour so Jenny knew each minute counted. She had to order, eat and get back to school before the bell rang.

"Next," said a voice from the counter. It was difficult to hear let alone talk over the noise from teens yelling and calling each other names.

"A burger and a diet coke please," Jenny requested but had to repeat it a couple of times due to the noise.

"Can I borrow a couple of bucks?" Jacy asked.

"Sure," she replied, but looked at him oddly. She really did not know this guy. She would be too embarrassed to ask for money from someone she did not know. "Let me put it on my order."

"Hey, thanks," Jacy said smacking his lips. "Can you add a medium fries and a coke?"

"What?" The cashier yelled cupping his ear.

"A medium fries and small coke."

The fellow behind the counter nodded and quickly got their food. Grabbing their trays, they scanned the restaurant for a table. She had never seen a McDonald's so full with teenagers, some even sitting on tabletops.

"Come on," Jacy yelled popping a fry into his mouth. "We can walk back and eat along the way."

Jenny nodded and followed him out of the restaurant. Rather than talk, they walked and ate until they found Jacy's friends. Gary stood smoking with his eyes closed. When he exhaled, he held the butt to his lips again. A sweet smell surrounded them and Jenny knew it was not an ordinary cigarette. He exhaled again before offering it to her.

"Want a drag?" He asked smiling. "This is good stuff."

Without warning, he stepped closer inviting her to take it. Jenny moved backward to increase the distance between them.

"Is that what I think it is?" She asked as a group of girls laughed aloud.

"What do you think I'm smoking?" Gary asked staring straight into her eyes.

"Grass." She said staring right back at him.

"Okay, so you aren't stupid," he smirked. "Now, do you want some?"

Peering across the street Jenny spotted the police officer walking along the sidewalk. She quivered at the fact that she was standing amid a group of teenagers passing around a joint. The officer glanced their way and she quickly turned her face.

"Aren't you afraid of getting in trouble?" She asked.

Gary followed her gaze and replied laughing, "You mean Officer Pete?" Passing the joint to Amanda he added, "We got an agreement. We don't smoke on school grounds, and he leaves us alone."

Jenny was shocked by his response, stared down at her feet and noticed the patches of grass covered with butts. *How anyone could deny smoking marijuana with all of the evidence around them?* She wondered. *If the officer came over, would I be just an innocent bystander?*

Jenny knew she should carefully choose her friends or she might get labeled as one of them. She glanced at her watch and realized that lunchtime would be over in five minutes.

"Got to get to class," she said before strolling away from the group. She turned to leave and to her surprise, they did not follow or try to stop her. As the day dragged on, she went from class to class but could not help thinking about the deal they had with the police officer. She knew it was illegal for anyone to smoke under the age 18 let alone grass yet this man turned his head.

As the week went by, Jenny grew accustomed to Jacy calling out to her as she passed the group on her way to McDonald's. They seemed to accept her for who she was and did not judge her.

I guess I shouldn't judge them either, she thought. At least I've got some friends to talk with during lunch.

§

Jenny never crossed paths with her sister Kristina since freshmen and sophomores went to one building, while juniors and seniors went to another. Kristina excelled at school and particularly liked arithmetic. Eric was in Grade 8 and found learning difficult so she often helped him with his homework. He tried asking their mother but she said in her day, they only needed two years of math so algebra was like a foreign language to her. Jessica, who was in the sixth grade always got into Jenny's belongings and tried on her clothes – something that really annoyed her. Then there was Regina, the baby of the family who was in Grade 3.

After a couple more weeks in their new home, everyone fell into their own routines. Since their parents were both employed, Jenny and Kristina took turns preparing dinner on nights when their mother worked late, and a list of chores was provided that were rotated each week. Jenny's days became consumed with school, homework and chores. Whenever her family was able to get together for dinner, say prayers, eat, and talk about their day, Jenny was happy.

5. Family Night

The cool fall weather changed the leaves into amazing hues of red, orange and yellow, and the petunias still maintained their colorful blooms. Jenny loved the changing of the seasons because it meant time was moving on and she was getting older. She had so many things to look forward to: turning 16 and getting a driver's license. Once she passed her driving test, she could ride in her friend's car without her parents getting upset and when she received her permit, she could drive her own car and hang out with her friends.

At school, Jenny grew to enjoy both her classes and her new friends. She felt more comfortable walking with Jacy to Mickey D's and thankfully, he did not always want to bum money. One Friday though, he did.

"Hey, Jen," he said as they walked into the restaurant dodging the rolled up napkins flying through space.

"Yes, I know," she replied laughing. "You want me to lend you money for fries even though you know you'll never pay me back."

Jacy rolled his eyes. As usual the line was long and filled with crazy freshmen throwing salt and pepper packets around. Of course they were opened so white and brown specks soon covered the floor. Just then the manager appeared and yelled at them. He threatened to make them leave, and never to be allowed in again.

As they waited for their order Jacy asked, "What are you doing tonight?" Jenny was still rapt by the drama unfolding in front of her and did not answer. A couple of teens left in a huff, while an employee came out with a broom to sweep the floor. Actually, Jenny just pretended not hear him.

The routine of walking back to the group while eating became normal so with drinks in one hand and food in the other, they left to find their friends. As usual they walked and ate in silence. She loved the fact that Jacy did not feel the need to talk all the time.

"So," he asked as they neared the group, "how about it?"

"What are you talking about?" She replied swallowing a bite of her burger. She knew full well what he meant but hoped he would not ask again.

"Do you want to go out with us tonight?"

"What are you guys doing?"

"We're just gonna hang out."

Jenny was not sure how to answer him. There was no way that her parents would let her spend time with those teenagers. If they knew she hung out with them at lunchtime, they would flip. The kids were courteous enough but their habits would never be acceptable. Anyway, Friday night's schedule consisted of pizza and movies at home. That was how it had always been in her family. The only one who left the tradition behind sometimes was Kristina because of her job. Jenny took the last bite of her burger, shoved the wrapper into the bag and took a sip of her drink.

"Not sure," she replied, staring at her cup and playing with the straw. She could sense his eyes on her and knew he wanted an explanation.

"My family usually has plans," she whispered.

"Yeah? Sounds like fun," he said sarcastically, and popped more fries into his mouth. "Probably a lot more exciting than hanging out with us," he added putting his finger to his cheek. "Mommy and daddy, and the rest of the family probably watching some Disney movie."

Jenny felt warmth creep up her neck and into her face. Embarrassed by his words, she turned away from him. *How dare he talk to me that way*, she thought.

When she started to walk away Jacy grabbed her arm. She stopped voluntarily but kept her eyes on her feet. Shuffling back and forth, she waited for him to speak again.

"Come on," he begged with an arrogant smile. "Please? You'll have fun. Trust me."

Jenny looked up at him puzzled. The obvious answer would be no but his eyes burned into hers making it impossible to argue. She rubbed the back of her neck as if deep in thought but did not reply. Jacy then turned on his heels and left to meet his friends.

"I'll ask," she said breathlessly, as she tried to catch up with him. "That's all I can do."

"Good," he said smiling widely. "We'll be down the street by my apartments. You can meet us at six o'clock."

Catching the bus after school, Jenny decided to forget their conversation. Her parents would want to meet whomever she hung around with but she knew those teens would be placed on their most 'unwanted list.' She could never arrange to meet them because her parents would not allow it.

§

Friday night began with the usual routine. Dad brought

home three large pizzas and the smell overtook the house making everyone hungry. Kristina placed paper plates on the coffee table and mom pulled a movie out of a small bag. As the opening credits rolled, Kristina spoke up.

"Hey mom, did you hear what happened today?"

Marie noticed distress in her eyes and the seriousness of her voice. She shook her head.

Kristina took a deep breath to keep tears from filling her eyes. "Two kids died at school today." The news was so stunning that everyone turned to stare at her.

"At school?" Asked Jenny, breaking the silence.

Kristina moved unsteadily to the couch and sat down. Her body trembled as she recalled what happened. She noticed students in the hallways crying in huddles. A friend knew a friend and so on until someone told her the sad news. "Some teens had driven to the mall during lunchtime even though they only had an hour," she said.

"On their way back to school they rushed, and reached the railroad tracks just as a train was coming. They knew that if they got stuck behind the train, they would have to wait anywhere from five to twenty-five minutes. They thought they could beat it… but didn't make it. They took the risk and lost their lives. The rumor circulated that this was not the first incident of a train hitting a car during lunchtime."

Mom dropped heavily into her chair. The images in her mind were too much to handle. She had noticed the tracks by the school but never thought about anyone getting hurt there, let alone teenagers losing their lives. *Why would anyone build a school so close to railroad tracks?* She wondered.

Jenny could not believe what she was hearing and a shiver ran down her back. This incident was the closest to death that she ever experienced. Nevertheless, she was intrigued and wanted to know more.

"Did you know any of them?" She asked.

"I hate the idea of the open campus at your school," Marie responded with tears in her eyes. Images of her own children crossing the tracks with a train coming made her tremble with fear. She wiped her wet cheeks with her hands.

"I can't even imagine how their parents are dealing with this," she said. *How could a school let this happen?* She wondered. *Well, we can settle one thing here and now. My kids will never drive there during school hours!*

"Mm, pizza," said Erik entering the living room. He took one look at his mother and added, "You okay, mom?"

Regina and Jessica soon joined the rest of the family. They each grabbed a slice of pizza and found seats to watch the movie.

"What movie did you get?" Asked Erik.

Mom wiped her eyes again and sniffled loudly before answering.

"The Dark Crystal," she said quietly.

"What's it about?" Jessica asked.

"I'm not sure," said Marie, "but I read that this movie has a good group called the Mystics and a bad group called the Skeksis. It's something about a missing shard of crystal that is needed to put balance back into the universe."

Marie tried to put the train scenario into the back of her mind. She wanted to enjoy this time with her family.

"Is it scary?" Asked Regina.

"I don't think so."

"Awe, shucks. I love scary movies," Erik noted, pizza in hand nestled on the floor by the couch.

"Sorry, but the man at the video store said we wouldn't

be disappointed."

Erik moaned, while the girls giggled with excitement.

6. Jacy's Bold Move

About 20 minutes into the movie there was a knock at the door, and mom rose to answer it. "Can I speak to Jenny please?" asked the dark-haired teen.

Jenny froze when she recognized his voice, and mom let him in. "I'm Jacy Kavi," he said.

Much to her surprise, he wore jeans and a buttoned up shirt with short sleeves that showed off his muscular arms. His hair was neatly combed and pulled back into a ponytail. Aware that he must be on his best behavior, Jacy reached out to shake Marie's hand. Then he walked up to Jim and shook his hand too. He knew that when he used good manners, parents tended to trust him. He introduced himself as a sophomore at Jenny's high school and asked how they liked Oklahoma. He added that someday, he'd like to visit Indiana.

"Where are your manners?" Marie said looking at Jenny.

"Want to sit and have pizza with us?" She asked.

With a loud sigh, Erik paused the movie. Jacy smiled and winked at Jenny before he answered.

"Actually, I came over to invite you out for a while," he said. Smiling, he turned to face her parents. Jenny's eyes shot up pleadingly to her mother but she looked to her dad for an answer.

"Where are you going?" He asked.

"My house," Jacy replied. "We're watching a movie too."

"And where do you live?"

"Just down the street. I walked here."

"Fine, only with one condition," he said sternly. "She must be home by 10 p.m." He glared at Jacy hoping to frighten him a little, but he showed no fear.

"No problem, sir."

Jenny quickly stood up to join him. She could not believe what just happened, but wanted to get out of there before they changed their minds.

"Thanks!" She said as they rushed out the door.

They flashed a smile to each other as they walked briskly down the street toward his apartment. When they reached the building, they went around it to the parking lot where a car waited for them. Inside sat Sandy, Susan, Amanda and Gary. Jacy opened the back door and jumped inside but Jenny hesitated. They just told her parents they would be at Jacy's.

"Come on," he coaxed. "Everything will be fine."

Even though her head told her no, she slid into the back seat next to him. As they drove down the street, Jenny tried to ignore the lie she just told. Before she knew it, they were out of the neighborhood and on the city's main streets. The radio blared loudly and the fun began.

At a stoplight the car doors opened, the teens jumped out of the vehicle and ran around it yelling frantically. Jacy grabbed Jenny's hand and pulled her out to join them. She tried to resist, but he was too strong. She stumbled over her feet as she kept her legs stiff trying to fight back. She was afraid when she saw the cars parked around them waiting for the light to change. When the light turned green they screamed and climbed back inside – something Jenny was more than happy to do. Laying rubber, the car made it through the green light just before it turned red again. Jenny's heart had never beaten so fast, and her breathing quickened. She had never laughed so hard in her life.

"What just happened?" She gasped excitedly.

"A Chinese fire drill," Jacy replied laughing.

The plan was to hang out at Amanda's house. Her parents were out for the evening so they would have the house all to themselves. The living room was complete with a couch, love seat and two recliners. Amanda brought out some chips and beer. Flopping into one of the recliners, Gary grabbed the TV remote. After he lit a cigarette, he took the ashtray off the table and placed it on the chair next to him so he could relax and drink his beer.

Jenny sat on the couch but did not feel comfortable. She knew she shouldn't be there. Sandy and Susan fought over what to watch on TV, which reminded Jenny of her sisters. When they found Grease, they agreed to watch it. Jacy grabbed a bowl of chips, salsa and two beers, and plopped down on the couch next to her.

"Here," he said handing her a can.

"No thanks."

She did not drink or smoke and she would not let him pressure her into it. Jacy just grinned and got up. He came back with a can of coke smiling, she willingly accepted. However, the first sip took her by surprise.

"Yuck," she said making a face. "What's in this?"

Susan, Sandy and Amanda, who were drinking beer looked at her distorted face and laughed aloud.

"Rum and coke," Jacy said snickering uncontrollably. "Come on, loosen up a little."

"I don't drink," she reminded him. Jenny gave him a

stern look and handed the glass back to him. He took the drink back to the kitchen and poured another with just a little rum hoping she could not taste it. After all, the salsa and chips did make her thirsty. She gave this one a try and seemed satisfied.

"I only put in a little rum," he said.

It was true that the first one had only a little, but as the night went on he made the drinks stronger and stronger. The more chips and salsa she ate, the thirstier she got, and the more she drank. Her tongue seemed to burn from the salsa and soon she could not even taste the rum.

They had settled in to watch the movie and Jacy leaned in close to her. Then he took her hand in his. She stiffened at first, but as the drinks took effect and everyone seemed to be having a great time, she began to relax. After a while, everything seemed funny and everyone laughed a lot.

When the movie ended, Jenny stood up, but quickly sat down again. Her head felt dizzy and she leaned back on the couch. She hadn't noticed it before, but the smoke in the room suddenly made her nauseous.

"Are you okay?" Jacy asked helping her up.

With his assistance she stumbled to the car and he got her home only a few minutes late. She thanked him and quietly tip toed into the house. She held her breath, hoping not to get caught. As she made her way to the bathroom, her mother startled her.

"You're late," she said, but Jenny ignored her. She shut the door quickly behind her and rushed to hug the toilet.

7. The Apology

Jacy was a sophomore in high school, and lived with his mother after his parents divorced. His father was a full blood Indian, and lived on the reservation. His mother was known as a pale face to his dad, and lived in town. Jacy felt like an outcast with his olive skin, long dark hair, and hairless chest. His mother, a sweet and gentle lady, worked full time at a nursing home from 3 to 11 p.m. as a nurse's aide to support him. While she was gone, he was left alone and learned to fend for himself. He needed to survive, and quickly realized that he could only count on himself.

It came as no surprise that he became a rebel at a young age. Not a bad one, but he would sneak out of the house, smoke with his friends, and occasionally drink if any of them bought beer. Unfortunately as he got older, he began smoking grass and if he could get something stronger in his grips, he more than happily got high.

He noticed Jenny a few days after school started. Although he knew he might not be her type, he could not help admiring her. He liked what he saw - a cute, quiet, polite and kind person. She was not like the other girls in town. Her shyness and how easy it was to make her blush captivated him. She was not a part of the popular crowd, but he wanted to get to know her. He usually dazzled any girl he wanted, but Jenny was not overwhelmed by his charm. She was a little harder to understand than the rest, and he willingly accepted the challenge.

At first he tried to get Jenny's attention while walking through the halls, but she never seemed to acknowledge him. He wondered if she was purposely ignoring him. Usually the new girls, the freshmen, would jump at the chance when he came around. He knew he was good looking with an adorable smile, but this time he had to plan and scheme to get this girl's attention. He finally asked Sandy to befriend her so he could meet her. He knew that if they could give her a ride home, he could find out where she lived. And it all worked out so easily. Jacy chuckled to himself, remembering how shy she was and how she turned so red.

It took a degree of courage for him to go to Jenny's house that night, but he wanted more than anything to hang out with her. To his surprise and delight, her parents seemed naïve. They knew nothing about him, but let her take off with him for the evening. He thought it was funny how he could act so politely and say the right words to be accepted. He was happy with the way things worked out. Now that he dangled the worm, he planned to catch this fish.

Jenny was sick as a dog all day Saturday, and did not feel a whole lot better on Sunday. She never drank alcohol before, and although she enjoyed the buzz it provided, she definitely did not like the after affects. First there was the upset tummy and headache. Then nausea took over with that aching feeling of her food trying to come back up the way it went down. She could not eat and the room spun whenever she moved. Thankfully, her mom thought she had the flu and nursed her back to health.

The following Monday, Jenny could not wait to get back to school.

"Hi, Jacy," she chirped as she sauntered toward the group at lunchtime.

He did not have to flag her down this time and he smiled, pleased with himself. Sandy, Susan, Amanda and Gary stood with him.

"Hi, Amanda," she said waving to the rest of the group.

Amanda looked at her with glazed eyes and an odd smile on her face. Gary sucked in slow inhales holding his roach in the middle of his hand. At one time, that would have bothered Jenny, but she was getting use to seeing it. In fact, she grew to accept this behavior as normal from them whether right or wrong. She quit looking for Officer Pete, also accepting that this man of the law just did not care.

"How are you today?" Jacy asked scanning her body. *Damn, she looks good*, he thought. He smiled as he recalled the first time he got hammered and how he threw up for a couple of days.

"Hungry," she said pulling at his shirt, urging him to follow her to Mickey D's.

Jacy enjoyed the attention, and realized that he was finally winning her over. As he followed her lead, the wind blew his long hair across his face. He quickly pushed it behind his ears and attempted to keep up with her pace.

"Did you get in trouble?" He asked.

A group of teens pushed past them as they chased each other trying to get to McDonald's first. One accidentally nudged Jenny's shoulder while zipping past her. Unsteadied by the sudden move she wavered for a second, but managed to keep her balance.

"Hey!" Jacy yelled throwing up his hand to offer a finger.

"I was too sick to get in trouble," Jenny giggled. "I

threw up, and my mom made me go to bed. She figured I must have the flu, so I slept most of the weekend."

"What a bummer," he smirked. "Oh, well. At least you didn't get caught for drinking."

Jenny placed a hand on her tummy as they continued to walk. She recalled how her entire body ached, how her stomach gurgled, and how her esophagus hurt as the acid climbed up to her throat making it burn with the yucky tasting liquid that filled her mouth. Then she'd vomit, but nothing came out. She never wanted to go through anything like that again.

"I never threw up so much before," she said. "I felt terrible."

"What did you think would happen if you couldn't hold your liquor?" Jacy laughed.

Her eyebrows lowered over her nose and he laughed even harder. "What do you mean?"

"Well, you had a few of those rum and cokes, and I made them kind of strong," he chuckled.

All color drained from Jenny's face. She could not believe what she heard. "Why would you do something like that?" She demanded.

"Hey," he replied defensively, "I just wanted you to loosen up and have some fun."

Jenny's body tensed and her mouth dropped into a frown. She glared at him and tried to think back, but could not remember how many drinks she had. She did remember that after a couple of them, they did not seem to taste so bad anymore. *How dare he make me sick*, she thought.

"What an awful thing to do," she said seriously. "I thought that I could trust you."

Jenny's eyes flashed straight ahead, and her legs marched off quickly trying to leave him behind. However he caught up and put his arms around her waist, stopping her from taking another step. She pushed his arms off, and stomped on ahead.

"Come on," he pleaded behind her. "You know I would never let anything bad happen to you, don't you?"

She stopped abruptly and turned to face him - her eyes piercing into his. "The fact that I threw up doesn't seem to bother you."

"Jenny, everyone throws up the first time," he said, his face softening. "You should have seen me the first time I got drunk. I hugged the toilet for a couple of days. I even put my pillow on the bathroom floor and slept there in between heaving." Jacy laughed releasing her eyes, remembering his first time.

"I don't think that's fun," Jenny grumbled closing her eyes for a second, and shaking her head. She turned around and headed again for McDonald's, which was by then just a few feet in front of her.

"Forgive me?" He asked, his dark brown eyes searching hers.

She ignored him, walked inside, and got in line. It seemed shorter than usual, which was a good thing since it had seemed to take longer just to get there. Even though some kids shouted while others threw Ketchup packages, it did not stop Jacy from taking her hand in his and gazing into her eyes. He knew she was going to be a challenge, and he willingly accepted it even though it was out of character for him to chase any girl. Finally their turn came up at the register, and as she ordered her lunch, she automatically added fries and drink for Jacy.

"Thank you," he responded. "It won't happen again."

"Promise?" She asked looking back at him. She looked so innocent, obviously wanting to believe him.

"I promise," he said.

8. A Different Family Night

Jenny knew that drinking and smoking was inappropriate. She was raised to know right from wrong, and thanks to regular church visits, she also knew how to care for and treat the body as a temple. When she was younger and playing in the park with Ashley, she would run away when other kids arrived at the park smoking, and tried to coax them to do the same. She had always followed the rules, but so much had changed since those carefree, innocent days. Of course, she was upset because her parents forced her to move out of state, and away from her best friend. Perhaps she was acting out - rebellious actions for making her life miserable.

She had difficulty making new friends, and did not feel accepted in her new school. Then Sandy came along. She seemed to be the only person who actually acknowledged her, and the only one who noticed that she was unhappy. The first time she accepted a car ride frightened her. It was also the first time she knowingly disobeyed her parents. She made sure they dropped her off by Jacy's apartment so none of her siblings would recognize her in the car. She was learning deceitfulness.

However, the second time she got into the car it seemed much easier, and she dismissed her uneasy conscience. She learned to enjoy the Chinese fire drill, and laughed along with the others whenever they did it. Other cars honked their horns when they tried to get back inside before the light turned red. It was like she'd awakened from a dream or a deep sleep. She discovered a different kind of world - an exciting one that she wanted to learn more about.

The following Friday at lunch, Jacy asked her to go out with them again. As he leaned against a tree with his legs crossed, he made circles with the smoke coming out of his mouth.

"I'd better not," she said. "It worked last week, but I'm pretty sure it isn't going to fly two weeks in a row."

Jacy took her hand and traced it with his fingers. "Are you sure?" He asked gazing at her admiringly.

Jenny felt goose bumps move up her arm and bit her lower lip before she answered.

"How about you come over to my house tonight?"

Jacy let her hand go and frowned – an obvious no. She wondered why she even asked him that. Her parents might not like him, and he might not like her family.

"Why would I want to do the family thing?" He asked.

Embarrassed, a hurtful frown crossed Jenny's face. "To spend time with me," she said weakly.

Although amused by her naivety, Jacy had no intention of spending the evening with her family. His mother never spent time with him, so what was the point? In fact, it sounded quite boring, but as his eyes sank into hers, he knew he had to see her somehow.

"Another day in paradise," he said taking her hand and squeezing it tight.

"Is that a yes?" She asked, her eyes wide open with anticipation.

"What time do you want me to come over?"

"Same as last week."

"See you tonight," he grinned.

On the bus home that day Jenny did not hear a word from the noisy kids, only the thoughts in her head. Jacy had agreed to come over! She could not get home fast enough and when she did, she rushed to her room to tidy up. She quickly picked up the books and magazines from the living room as well. Her heart pounded with expectation.

"Come on Erik, Jessica-- please put your books in your rooms," she pleaded. Taking out the vacuum cleaner, she ran it over the carpet. She also dusted the furniture and made sure the room was tidy for company.

"What's the big occasion?" Asked Kristina before she left for work. "You usually make mom beg you before you clean anything up."

As Kristina left the room, Jenny stuck her tongue out at her – a habit still from childhood. When she finished cleaning, she waited impatiently for mom and dad's car to pull up. When she saw them turn into the driveway, she ran out to greet them.

"Mom," she asked in a high-pitched voice, "Is it all right if Jacy comes over tonight?" Dad handed three boxes of pizza to her, the door slammed shut, and they made their way inside.

"The boy who came over last week?" Marie asked.

"Yes," she replied anxiously crossing her fingers behind her back.

Jenny was ecstatic, but tried to keep her composure. She recalled the weekend before and knew her parents would frown on her being friends with Jacy if they learned what *really* happened that night.

At that same moment, Jacy answered a knock at his door, and opened it to see Gary smiling with a six-pack of beer in hand. Immediately, they both lifted their right hands and slapped them high in the air.

"Hey man, you're here," he said taking the beer from his friend and placing it on the table. Tearing open the carton he took out a can. "It's cold, cool."

"Yeah, my old man had them in the fridge," Gary replied opening a can for himself. "I just asked for one but he offered the whole pack."

They plopped onto the couch and Gary started playing with the television remote. He scanned through the channels looking for something to watch while Jacy lit himself a cigarette.

"So what are the plans for tonight?" Gary asked tossing his empty can into the garbage, and grabbing another one off the table.

Jacy took a long inhale before opening his mouth and emitting circles of smoke. They both laughed as they inspected the circles in the air.

"Going to Jenny's tonight," he replied, twitching his nose. "Going to do the *family* thing."

"Sounds totally boring," Gary replied flashing his eyes at him, and taking another sip of beer.

Jacy figured he would wind up feeling uncomfortable sitting with Jenny's family for the evening, so he decided to start partying early. He thought that if he had a couple of beers in him, he could stay on his best behavior and get through the evening. With a change of clothes and some gum, no one would be the wiser.

He arrived right on time and like any father, Jenny's dad wasted no time asking questions.

"So where does your dad work," Jim asked after offering him a slice of pizza.

"Sir, he lives on the reservation and I live here in town with my mother."

"I'm sorry," Jim responded. "So your parents are divorced?"

"Yes sir. I do see my dad, but not all the time."

"And your mom... what does she do?"

"She works at the Park Regency as a nurse's aide."

"Do you plan on going to college?"

"I want to, sir but I'm not sure if I'll have the money?"

"Have you thought of a scholarship?" Jim asked.

When the interrogation ended, the evening became more palatable. Jacy envied how Marie and Jim sat beside each other, sharing loving glances every now and then. He even caught Jim giving Marie a kiss on the cheek. He noticed how the kids reacted at different parts of the movie, sometimes getting loud, screaming or laughing. He chuckled as the two youngest ones, Jessica and Regina, fought with each other. Jessica noticed the last piece of pizza on the plate and decided to take it without asking anyone if they wanted to share. Regina had the same idea and they both grabbed the piece together.

"It's mine," Regina shouted trying to rip the slice from Jessica's hands.

Jessica swiped Regina's arm trying to push her away. Regina grew angry and hit her shoulder. Jessica fell backwards; the pizza went flying in the air and then fell face down on the carpet. Then Marie yelled at both of them with a lecture about sharing. She made them apologize to each other, and insisted that they clean up the mess.

    This was all a part of home life that Jacy had never experienced and it seemed to make quite an impression on him. He glanced at Jenny as she watched the movie, and laughed with her siblings. He stared long enough to make her quickly turn her head for a second and smile before turning back to the TV. He realized that there was more to her than she let on, and he wanted to know all about her.

9. True Friends

The following week, Sandy asked Jenny to go shopping at the mall. She felt as if she had a new female friend. Of course Jenny was not allowed to ride with other teenage drivers so Marie dropped her off by the front doors. The parking lot was full, and people streamed in past her. Although somewhat embarrassed, she wanted to go so she agreed with mom's rules.

"See you at three o'clock sharp right here, sweetie," Marie said giving her daughter a peck on the cheek.

She had planned to meet Sandy in front of the Gap. In the crowded mall hallways, mothers pushed strollers with crying babies, and small children walked quickly beside their parents trying to keep up. In the middle of the halls were booths with people selling mobile phones and jewelry. Jenny searched for the Gap and her friends. Sandy happened to notice her first and waved. She was with Amanda and Susan outside the store. Then they went inside to look at the clothes and shoes on the racks.

Jenny enjoyed being with the girls and checking out the clothes together, trying things on, and giving opinions on how they thought they looked. The girls tried on sunglasses and checked out the jewelry. Then Susan decided it was time to eat, so they hurried to the food court. The number of food venders made it difficult to choose from, but Jenny picked pizza and met the other girls back at the table. Music piped into the mall, and the voices of people all around gossiping made it noisy while they ate their meal.

They took a couple of bites before Susan opened her purse and pulled out a rhinestone bracelet. Jenny thought she recognized the piece from the last store they visited.

"How do you like it?" Susan asked as she slid the bracelet onto her arm. She twirled it around making the stones sparkle and glitter. Jenny gawked at the price tag, which still hung from it.

"Where did you get that?" She questioned firmly.

"Easy, a five finger discount," Susan replied nonchalantly.

She appeared calm as Amanda and Sandy admired the bracelet. They did not seem bothered by what she said, but Jenny nervously scanned the area for mall police.

"You shoplifted?" Jenny asked surprised. "If you didn't have the money and wanted it that bad, why didn't you ask one of us to get it for you?"

"What kind of fun would that be?" Susan smirked as she passed it to Sandy. "I shoplift for the thrill of it."

Jenny immediately lost her appetite and stopped eating. She could not believe what she heard.

"Have you ever gotten caught?" She asked curiously.

Susan looked up and paused as if in thought. "Yes, actually I did get caught once," she said between bites.

"What happened?"

"Not much," she said in a cocky tone. "It was my first time, and the store manager didn't press any charges… so I got off."

Amanda and Sandy smiled at Susan while Jenny sat puzzled and more than a little stunned. "So you got off but you didn't get scared enough to never steal again?" She asked trying to understand.

"What's the worst thing you've ever done?" Susan asked turning the conversation around.

Jenny was startled by her question and her mind drew a blank.

"I drove home once drunk as a skunk," offered Amanda.

"And?" Asked Susan as if to say, *so what?*

"A cop passed me on the road, and I was scared shitless." She had everyone's attention as she continued. "But I kept my cool and he didn't stop me."

She paused as her mind replayed the incident. She had attended a party where her parents did not know she would drink. She remembered tripping down the front steps and stumbling into her car. It was difficult to slide the key into the ignition, but she finally got it started. As she drove home, she could not distinguish the lines on the road so she slowed down. When she finally reached her street, she saw a police officer and pressed the gas pedal. As a result, she sped a little too fast up the driveway. The car squealed and all of a sudden, she saw a beige wall in front of her. Quickly, she slammed on the brakes. The car jerked to a stop sending her flying forward.

"I think I hit the garage door," she giggled, "but I told mom I had no idea how the dent got on the door."

Jenny gasped.

"My turn," Sandy insisted. "I have to say the worse thing I guess is… can you keep a secret?" She put her first finger to her lips, as everyone's eyes remained glued to her face. "Are you sure? I don't want this to get around."

They took their fingers and acted like they were zippering their lips and throwing away the key.

"Okay, I'm not a virgin."

Jenny's eyes opened wide, she felt her jaw fall and slowly closed her mouth.

"Who was it?" Amanda asked, her hand covering her mouth.

"I don't kiss and tell," laughed Sandy.

"Your turn," Susan said turning her attention to Jenny.

She responded by twisting uncomfortably in her seat. *What could she say?* She tried all her life to behave, and not get into trouble. She closed her eyes for a moment trying to think of something she did wrong. She sensed all of their eyes on her. *Think. Think,* she thought. *It could be the Friday night when her parents thought she was at Jacy's house and to top it off, I got drunk,* but to this bunch of friends, that would not be viewed as a bad thing. Then it came to her, something she was ashamed of herself for doing.

"I guess the worse thing I…" she paused and cleared her throat before she went on. She placed her hands behind her back and crossed her fingers. "I wore my sister's favorite shirt to school without telling her. Ink spilled making a terrible stain. I tried to wash it off but couldn't, so I threw the shirt away. Until this day, she has no idea what happened to it."

To Jenny, her actions were reprehensible and something she hid deep inside her soul. To her new friends, however, this brave announcement amounted to nothing. The girls sat quietly for a few minutes slurping their drinks.

"You never shoplifted?" Probed Susan.

Jenny shook her head and Susan rolled her eyes as if disgusted by her frivolous confession.

"And I don't suppose you ever got drunk?" Challenged Amanda with a loud sigh.

"Jacy said I was drunk at your house last week," she

said hopefully.

"You were high. You were not drunk dear," Amanda clarified.

Feeling ill at ease, Jenny shrugged her shoulders.

"I don't even have to ask if you ever made out with a boy before, *do I?*" Asked Sandy.

Jenny stiffened in her seat. She did hold hands with Jacy the other day: BORING. "Whatever," she replied tensely. "There are other ways to have fun without getting into trouble."

§

"What are you doing tonight?" Asked Sandy. "Want to go out and have some real fun?"

Jenny felt apprehensive and more than a little confused. She had no idea where these girls were coming from, and what kind of lives they led. The only knowledge she had about them was what she learned the other day at the mall. Susan was a shoplifter, Amanda got drunk, and Sandy was no longer a virgin, but as with everyone, there was a story behind each of these girls' lives, and it would take some time before Jenny learned the truth.

She ascertained that Amanda's home life was less than desirable. Granted, her parents were still together and had plenty of money. In fact, they bought her a new Chevrolet, but they occupied their time with various organizations and groups, always promoting and too busy for their daughter. She did not know what it was like to have a home cooked meal, or watch a movie on a Friday night with her parents.

They owned a large house with a bar in the basement full of liquor. They had parties with music and drinking, and it was not uncommon for them to imbibe into the wee hours. Amanda would find them passed out in the morning.

It was also customary for them to let Amanda drink with them. They said as long as she was at home under their supervision, drinking was acceptable. Partly because of the late night parties, and the times she missed school due to hangovers, she needed to repeat the tenth grade. If it were not for Susan and Sandy, she would have been lonely. They had become not only her best friends but also her surrogate family.

Susan, the oldest of her sibling, lived at home where money was scarce. Her parents were divorced, and her mom worked full time to put food on the table. Her dad visited once a week and they got their checks, but her brother grew like a weed. Her mother struggled to keep them all dressed and their tummies full. Susan loved her brother and took care of him during the evenings when her mom worked. She knew how to make simple meals like Mac and cheese or hot dogs. She had engaged in much more shoplifting than she let on, only she did not get caught. In fact, that's how she acquired her eye makeup and new earrings, amongst other things. Her mother definitely could not afford them.

Sandy's case was even more deplorable. Her parents divorced when she was a child. She did not know her father, and her mother always invited different boyfriends to live at their house. It seemed like each month she kicked one out, and a new one replaced him, so it became routine for her to encounter a different man when she came home from school.

About a year ago her mother had a young boyfriend who took an interest in Sandy. He hung around the house most of the time and Sandy enjoyed his company. She watched him drink and nibble on her mother's neck, before they excused themselves to the privacy of their bedroom. She had seen guys do this in the past. Sometimes, he sat in front of the television with Sandy and touched her softly on her back or knee. She thought little of it until one night when they had pizza and coke. He slipped something in her drink and before long her senses went awry. Her mind could not tell her arms or legs to move, and her head felt fuzzy.

Then he picked her up and placed her on her bed. She begged him to stop, but could not comprehend why her mouth was so uncooperative. He smiled as he removed her clothes and told her she was beautiful. His hands caressed her body while he kissed her and then he raped her.

Even her tears did not prompt him to stop. He left her lying naked, and she fell asleep that way unable to move. She told her mother the next day and she kicked him out, but the police were not called. This horrible incident was something she would have to live with for the rest of her life.

After everything they'd been through in their short lives, Amanda, Susan and Sandy seemed more self-assured and courageous than Jenny thought she could ever be. They appeared unafraid of life and she thought maybe - just maybe - she wanted to be just like them. She also knew that if her mother discovered their true selves, their friendship would be over.

10. A Family Thanksgiving

Over the following months Jenny grew accustomed to her new school and her new friends, as strange as they behaved at times. She looked forward to meeting Jacy every day and sometimes he watched television with her family on Friday nights. Once in a while, she lied so she could meet the gang at Jacy's for a night out.

On the day before Thanksgiving, Jenny stood in line at Mickey D's with Jacy and some other teenagers. In the middle of whooping and hollering students, they tried to talk about the four-day weekend coming up. Although they had become good friends, it sometimes felt as if it might be more - especially on the days he held her hand like he did on this particular day.

"Jacy," she said, "please join my family for Thanksgiving dinner." With their fingers intertwined, Jenny rubs one of his knuckles with her thumb. He just shook his head laughing.

"If you don't come, I won't see you for four days," she pleaded batting her long lashes at him.

"I got plans," he replied – an obvious lie and Jenny frowned.

"With whom?" She asked condescendingly. "Your mother? Will she cook turkey too?" Jacy quickly withdrew his hand – a sign that he resented both her words and the tone of her voice.

"My mom has to work on Thanksgiving," he said with a grimace. "Thank you very much." His face displayed his jealousy over Jenny having such a close-knit family. His stiffened features revealed his dismay over only having a mom. He did not seem angry about it, just hurt because no other family members cared enough to be there.

"That's her regular shift," he explained.

Jenny shifted from one leg to the other with her hands folded in front of her. Inside, she scolded herself for speaking to him so bluntly. The last thing she wanted was to upset him and his words grieved her heart.

"I will be on the reservation with my father," he continued in a matter of fact tone. "…and no turkey, thank you, we hunt deer."

Jacy recalled the last time he and his father went out to shoot a buck. They stood quietly by as a family of deer stopped for a drink. The scene was so peaceful that he could hear the wind rustle through the leaves. They dared not move or even breathe too hard for fear of scaring the deer away. Jacy struggled to hold his heavy rifle steady until his dad whispered, "Now." He aimed, slowly pulled the trigger and hit one of the deer in the forehead right between the eyes. The shrieking sound of the animal as it hit the ground was horrifying. Nonetheless, he became a good hunter over the years and it was a sport he truly enjoyed.

Jenny glanced up at Jacy and could see the hurt in his eyes.

"I'm sorry," she sighed. "I didn't mean it. I'm just going to miss you, that's all."

Jacy's face softened. He took her hand in his again and slowly withdrew her from the line. It had moved so slowly that some of the teens in the back asked others in the front to order for them, which took even longer.

Wait!" She laughed, yanking his arm to hold him back. "Look - there are only a couple of people ahead of us now."

But Jacy pulled her aside anyway and they exited through the side door. As he leaned against the buildings outside wall, he locked eyes with her.

"What's up?" Jenny asked.

Then he leaned in and kissed her softly on the lips. As her eyes closed, her body trembled. When he finally released her, she stumbled backward unaware of her surroundings. Her heart beat so fast that she feared she might hyperventilate. Although astonished and somewhat dazed by Jacy's unexpected action, she knew it was love that consumed her body and mind.

"Maybe this will last until we meet each other on Monday," he whispered softly. Then he drew her to him and kissed her again – deep and hard.

§

Thanksgiving morning arrived too soon like all holidays. The sun stood out brightly in a blue sky that fooled everyone into thinking the weather was warm. In reality, the thermometer only reached fifty degrees. There were many things to do before the Thanksgiving dinner. Food had to be readied; the house dusted, vacuumed and straightened up, dirty dishes put into the dishwasher and clothes washed. Marie prepared the turkey while Jim made the stuffing. The trimmings included broccoli with cheese, cranberries and spaghetti. The best part would be the dessert - three different kinds of pies.

While Jim and Marie cooked they were yelling orders to the kids.

"Don't forget to make your beds. Who's cleaning the bathroom? Don't forget to wash the bathtub. Make sure the clean clothes are folded and put away."

Jessica and Regina were glued to the television watching the Thanksgiving Day parade. Jenny vacuumed amid protests from the little ones that they could not hear the TV. Kristina took care of the laundry and Erik cleaned the bathrooms. By 1 p.m., they still had enough time to tidy the kitchen, set the table, and get dressed before their guests arrived at 3 o'clock. In this household, teamwork always saved the day.

Church members Tom and Thelma were invited for dinner. Tom, a short good-looking man with streaks of grey at his temples, was a church deacon and also loved tending to a beautiful flower garden in his back yard. Thelma was a stunning woman who never missed a week at the beauty salon. Her long white hair was turned up into a French twist. They were both in their 60's but never blessed with children. Since they had no family in town, Marie ensured that they could enjoy good food and company for the holiday.

When dinner was ready everyone surrounded the table, held hands and prayed. After they sat down, Jim carved the turkey.

"I've never heard of spaghetti for Thanksgiving?" Thelma said putting some noodles on her plate. "This smells so good."

"Ha ha," laughed Marie. "This is only what I know being brought up Italian. Always turkey and spaghetti."

"My favorite part of the meal is the stuffing," Tom noted glancing at his wife. "Did you cook it in the turkey?"

"I usually do that," said Thelma who leaned in to sniff a spoonful. "Corn bread stuffing that is... but this seems much different." Thelma squinted a little as she took in the tempting smell.

"Sorry, but I don't like cornbread stuffing, and I don't bake it inside the turkey," Jim said. Taking a bite of food he added, "I use Italian sausage. It's an old recipe my parents used."

"Mmm..." Thelma said taking a bite. "It's very good."

"So what does Thanksgiving really mean?" Jim asked out of the blue. He glanced at each one of his children to make sure they were paying attention.

"Easy," chirped Erik setting down his fork. "I'm thankful to have a roof over my head and this delicious food to eat."

"I'm thankful for my family," said Jessica. "Please pass the biscuits."

Jenny and Kristina rolled their eyes, and continued eating.

"I'm thankful your mother invited us over," Thelma smiled. "Everything's so good!"

"Thanks," Marie replied and passed a bowl of mashed potatoes around the table.

"Well, how did Thanksgiving start?" Jim asked.

"That's easy," Regina commented. "The pilgrims and the Indians started the tradition. The pilgrims boarded the Mayflower and ended up on some land where they had trouble surviving, so the Indians taught them how to live," she said with a proud smile. "In return they had Thanksgiving."

"Glad to hear you actually paid attention in school," said Kristina sarcastically. "Did you know they had wild ducks and geese for the first Thanksgiving – not turkey?"

"Yuck," Regina replied pinching her nose.

"Well, I think of how horrible we treated the Indians,

taking their land from them and all," Jenny noted with dismay.

Since Jacy's heritage was Native Indian, she naturally thought of him and wondered what he was doing. She also pondered if his people still held a grudge against the white folk for things that happened so long ago. As she ate the turkey, she envisioned him out hunting for his supper with his father.

"Very true," Tom said, "...but that's another story. The native people learned their ways from the earth, animals and plants. The white men came and imposed their European values on the Indians. For instance, they showed them how to use metal tools, plows and guns. Unfortunately, they also introduced them to strange diseases that they had no natural immunity against. They say more Indians died from diseases than were lost in war fighting for their homeland."

For a few moments everyone fell silent likely considering Tom's words. As forks scrapped the plates, Kristina glanced at Jenny who looked over at Jessica and Regina. They did not want a history lesson at the dinner table so they said nothing more on the subject.

"Do you have any family traditions from Thanksgiving?" Asked Erik, changing the subject. "As you can see, ours is turkey with Italian food."

"It's always wonderful to bring the whole family together," Jim added. "It was especially nice when the children's grandpa was alive. I wish you could have met him. He was such a character even into his old age." Jim paused for a second and stared into space as if drifting back in time.

"My mother had three sisters and two brothers," he continued. "All but one of them lived in town. When we got together there were so many of us that we set up tables in the kitchen, living room, and family room. Tables were set up in the garage for all the children. Afterward my grandpa always played his harmonica."

"How many people showed up?" Asked Erik inquisitively.

"I don't know," said Jim. "I never counted but a boat load of people to be sure. Imagine my mom's three sisters, one brother, husbands, wives and all their children."

"Sounds like a lot of fun," said Jessica.

"Wow," chuckled Regina. "Sounds so cool."

"Except for the cleaning up part after the meal," Kristina commented. "I bet that was a lot of work."

"Yep," Jenny added with a grin, "I wouldn't want to be on kitchen duty!"

"Anyone want seconds?" Marie asked putting more food on the serving dishes.

As Jenny scooped another serving of potatoes onto her plate, she thought of Jacy again on the reservation. She missed him and hoped he enjoyed this day with his father as much as she enjoyed hers with her family.

11. Sixteen And Confused

An attitude reflects a person's inner thoughts and their behavior is their outward expression of those thoughts. With that being said, a strong bond between friends can change their behavior. It is said that we become a product of our environment and even morals can be reshaped by our socialization within that environment. This is what seemed to happen to Jenny.

On a frigid December day, she waited for the guard at school to let her cross the street. On the other side Jacy lit a smoke and waved when he spotted her. Sandy, Susan and Amanda huddled in a circle trying to stay warm. Gary leaned casually against a tree looking quite stoned.

"Hey, Jacy," puffed Jenny as she ran to his side.

He exhaled and let the smoke come out of his nose. Then he put his arm around her pulling her close before kissing her gently.

"How's my girl," he asked handing her the lit cigarette.

Jenny grinned and took a long drag.

"Good now," she beamed, "and starving."

He took her hand and they headed to the fast food joint. The weather was so frigid that they decided to stay inside Mickey D's while they ate. Between noisy teenagers and all the full tables, they were forced to eat standing up by a window.

"Thanks again for the fries and drink," Jacy said

taking a sip of his soda.

"You're welcome," she replied between bites of her burger.

"Meet me after school?" Jacy asked.

"I don't think so?"

"Why not?"

"I don't want to get caught in Amanda's car."

"Please?" He begged with his big brown eyes.

She hated when he looked at her that way because she usually gave in and he would get his way. He leaned in and kissed her by her ear.

"Please?" He whispered again.

"Fine," she said reluctantly, "…but if I get caught, I'll hold you personally responsible."

Jacy smiled, drew her close and kissed her again. Jenny jabbed his rib jokingly, tossed her wrapper into a nearby bin and took off out the door. Jacy raced behind, caught up to her and spun her around. They were laughing aloud and kissed again. Although it seemed like the coldest day of the year, they did not seem to notice. What they felt for each other kept them more than a little warm.

After school she met Jacy in the parking lot and they scurried into the back seat of Amanda's car. He put his arm around her and kissed her passionately forgetting that anyone else was there.

"Gross," said Amanda peering at them through her rear view mirror. "Go get a room."

Gary sat in the front seat. He lit a joint and the sweet smell permeated the car. He drew in a long slow drag before passing it to Amanda. She did the same and handed it behind her to Jacy. Jenny glared at him with alarm, but he ignored her and did the same. Then he exhaled right into her face causing her to cough.

"Come on," he pleaded. "This stuff isn't going to hurt you. Just take one drag." She hesitated for a second as if actually considering the offer, and then shook her head no. To her surprise, Jacy then placed the joint between her lips and stared into her eyes – a bold move that startled and somewhat frightened her.

"Just a little drag," he begged. "For me?"

Jenny's eyes grew big as she considered his offer. If she refused Jacy might get angry. If she took just one drag it could put an end to the standoff. She let down her guard and took a puff.

"Breath in deep," he said obviously pleased with himself. With the joint between her lips, she sucked in and held it before she blew out the smoke.

"My turn," urged Gary leaning over in his seat.

Jacy was not about to part with it just yet. He coaxed Jenny to take another drag first. Then he leaned in, his lips found hers and molded into them. To his delight, Jenny grabbed him around his neck and drew him close kissing him hard. He knew marijuana could heighten the senses, especially the sense of touch but he had never seen her this way before. He figured the grass had something to do with it and definitely liked the change in her.

§

January brought more extreme cold with snow as well, but Jenny and Jacy always managed to keep each other warm inside. One day her mom rushed from the icy outdoors into the warmth of the house. Jenny was still in the shower when she entered with colorful helium balloons and a cake. This was a special day and her mom wanted to make it just right for her daughter. Kristina entered the steamy bathroom as Jenny stood with soap bubbles in her hair. Within seconds the mirror fogged up.

"Mom told me to tell you to hurry up, Jen," she said and then leaned down to flush the toilet.

"Oh!" Screamed Jenny. "Did you have to do that? The water is freezing!"

"Sorry, I forgot," she snickered. She went out the door but leaned back in to added, "You heard me, right? Mom wants you to hurry."

"I'll be out in a minute."

Goose bumps raced over Jenny's body while she waited for the water to warm back up. Finally her body relaxed under the hot water and she rinsed her hair. She had a big day ahead of her and wanted to look perfect.

Jessica and Regina were upset because their friends could not come to the event. Their mom reminded them it was Jenny's birthday not theirs.

"It's Jenny's day and we're going to celebrate it together as a family," Marie insisted. She truly believed it was important to celebrate the day a person came into this world because it was such an amazing gift. She said life was short and it was of utmost importance to enjoy it while we could.

"Can you help me braid my hair?" Kristina asked handing a brush, comb, and rubber band to her mother.

Even Erik dressed up for Jenny's big day, and finally everyone was ready. They grabbed their warm winter coats and left the house. They pulled into a parking lot with only a few other cars and they made their way toward two big front doors. Salt had been poured on the sidewalk in front to keep the ice away.

Once inside, they walked down a small corridor and pushed open a pair of swinging doors. These led them into a large room full of pool tables - at least ten of them - and a fully stocked bar at the end of the room. A handful of people stood at a couple of tables playing the game. The lights were dim and the sound of sticks hitting the balls cracked loud and quick. They moved on to another room with tables set up for meals and a couple of them were occupied. The manager noticed them and nodded for them to follow him to yet one more room. Inside was a long table by one wall and a couple of tables with chairs by a window. In the middle of the room stood a lone pool table. Marie set the cake on the long table along with a bag of balloons and streamers.

"Come on kids, we need to decorate before the guests arrive," she urged.

Kristina, Jenny and Erik blew up balloons and taped streamers across the room. Jim walked in behind them with the helium balloons and tied them to the chairs.

"What time do you want the pizzas to be ready?" The manager asked.

"I'm not sure yet," Marie replied. "Can I tell you after everyone have arrived?"

With snow still falling outside, she was not sure how many people would show up or even be on time. She pointed to the window and the manager followed her gaze.

"With the weather and all, I'd rather wait a bit."

"Of course," he agreed.

Jenny had handed out invitations all over school, but was not sure how many people, if any would actually attend but within the hour, the first guests walked in including a girl from her first class of the day.

"Mom, this is Lisa," she announced. "Lisa this is Marie."

"Nice gig," Lisa replied. "Who's all coming?"

"I don't really know," Jenny said shaking her head. "I didn't put RSVP on the invitations and with all the snow out there still coming down... it's hard to say."

"Yeah, my dad almost didn't let me come," she giggled. "I had to beg him."

About fifteen minutes passed before someone else showed up. After thirty more minutes, the room filled up with teenagers including Sandy, Susan, Amanda, Gary and Jacy.

"Good to see you again Marie," Jacy said politely. "May I introduce you to my friends?" While Marie shook hands with each of them, Jenny ran to Jacy's side and grabbed his hand.

"Hi," Jacy said sweetly squeezing her hand.

"Glad you made it," she replied excitedly. "I was afraid the snow might keep you from coming."

"You're kidding, right?"

Jacy closed the gap between them and brushed his lips softly across her cheek. Jenny blushed, noticed her mother's stare and quickly turned away. The look on Marie's face was enough to make her pull back and drop his hand. She had to behave normally and not let on how she felt for him, at least not in front of her parents.

Jacy grabbed a pool stick and played a game against Gary. Sandy, Susana and Amanda stood together checking out the clothes everyone was wearing. The music played with a few kids dancing, while others sat or stood gossiping. In no time, the aroma of pizza filled the air and the teens gathering around the table. The talking hushed as they popped food into their mouths, but when the noise arose again, Jim signaled for dessert.

"Okay, everyone," he shouted spying the empty pizza pans and soda cans. "May I have your attention please?"

The music stopped and immediately the lights dimmed. Marie emerged through the kitchen door with a birthday cake holding sixteen lit candles. Everyone's head turned with mumbles of how good the cake looked as she approached the table. She placed it in front of Jenny and began to sing Happy Birthday. Of course, everyone else joined in.

Jenny had to admit it that it was a great party. After another hour or so some of the teens said goodbye. Jacy turned to Jenny and told her he would see her at school on Monday. Before he left, he snuck in a kiss on her cheek leaving her with a broad smile.

By the time Jenny and her family left the pool hall several inches of snow covered the ground. A strong north wind blew the snow in circles around the car and repeatedly covered the windows with a thin layer of white. It was a treacherous drive home, but Jim drove slowly and they arrived home safely.

After thanking her parents for the party and kissing them good night, Jenny sat in the darkness of her room deep in thought. She still missed her friend Ashley and wished she could have been there for her big day. She listened as the wind howled outside of her window and considered how different her life had become. She stared out at the winter wonderland. The moon seemed so big staring out amid a few dark clouds. *I don't even know who I am anymore*, she mused.

Jenny thought of Jacy, confused about her feelings for him. She knew he was a rebel with no respect for authority, and was probably not good for her. Yet he was the only one that seemed to know and understand her. She reflected on some of the immoral things she did with him that she would never have considered on her own. She rationalized that he woke her up to life. Her parents kept a shield of protection over her and did not let her experience what the world had to offer. He told her he would never do anything to hurt her and she believed him.

12. The Rave Party

When February rolled around, the snow disappeared and it was unusually warm for that time of year - fifty degrees. A coat and hat was still needed but at least it was no longer freezing. Jacy had been pressuring Jenny to come out with him to a real party. Although he enjoyed her birthday party, he said he wanted to show her what a real party was like.

"There's so much fun and excitement in this life that you're missing," he said. "Please let me show you. You trust me don't you? I want you to experience all of this with me."

He used words like 'amazing' and 'exciting' to help wear her down. Then the day finally arrived when she was destined to give in. As they walked to Amanda's car after school, he tried to convince her. They walked with arms around each other and heard the last bell of the day ring loudly across the school grounds. Teenagers ran past them, yelling and screaming.

"How am I supposed to get out of the house that late?" Jenny asked.

"Easy," smirked Jacy squeezing her waist.

He glanced up and saw Amanda by her car waving to them. Jenny waved back.

"Hey Jacy, Jenny," Sandy shouted from behind. She ran past them and smacked Jacy playfully on the head.

"Hey!" He laughed leaning forward to try to swat her back.

"So what time are we leaving tonight?" Sandy asked clearly amused.

"About midnight," Jacy replied still trying to hit her. Sandy swatted him again and he loosened his grip from Jenny's waist. As she ran around him laughing, he tried to reach out to catch her.

"Jenny," Sandy sang whirling around them, "Are you coming?" Before she could answer they reached the car. Jenny entered first and Jacy scooted in next to her.

"What time do your parents go to bed?" Jacy asked.

"I dunno..." She replied shaking her head, "Maybe around tenish?"

"Good, so all you have to do is be real quiet and make your way out the front door." He paused for a moment knowing he should explain more clearly before she chickened out.

"They won't be any the wiser," he insisted. "You can sneak back in the same way. Really, it's a piece of cake."

Jenny shuddered at the thought.

"They'll be sleeping Jenny, and they'd never expect you to do something like that... so it's not like they'll be waiting for you to leave."

Jenny knew that part was true, but was not so sure about the rest. She had never done anything like that before.

Jacy saw her body tense up and her smile fade away. He had to think fast before she caved. "I will be outside waiting for you," he added reassuringly.

There were times when she got up about midnight to get a glass of water and her parent's bedroom door was shut. They never seemed to hear her but sneaking through the house and out the door was another matter entirely. Jacy smiled and his dark eyes met hers.

"You're gonna be all right," he said leaning in to plant a kiss on her lips. "We'll have so much fun."

Jenny's searched his face for the acceptance she needed. With one more prolonged and deep kiss, she knew what she had to do.

"Okay," she said taking in a deep breath. "I'll try."

At Jacy's apartment, Jenny got out and walked toward home. As she entered the front door, she felt nauseous in the pit of her stomach. Tossing her books on the couch, she ran to the kitchen to find a snack. Whenever she felt edgy, she got hungry. Pouring a glass of milk and grabbing some cookies from a jar on the counter, she sat, ate and felt a little better.

Since it was Friday, she knew it was family time. Before everyone assembled in the living room, she watched her two little sisters giggle at the cartoons on the television. The door to Erik's room was closed but the music from inside blared out. Kristina was nowhere to be found. The degree of Jenny's nervousness rose with each passing minute. Her heart pounding, she decided to grab her books and go to her room.

Why am I so uptight? She thought. It's going to be easy like Jacy said.

To calm herself down she lied on her bed and closed her eyes. About two hours later, everyone gathered in the living room as the movie of choice began to play. As usual, they ate pizza and talked. When the movie began, the little ones screamed with laughter. No one suspected just how anxious Jenny felt inside. However, she was quieter than usual – something that did not go unnoticed by her parents, and they asked her what was wrong. She simply said she was especially tired that evening and they seemed relieved.

About 10:30 p.m., the movie ended and everyone headed off to bed. Jenny put on her pajamas, got into bed and pretended to sleep. She heard her parents get into bed, but decided to rest a little longer – just to be sure. Then she sat up and clutched her blanket.

"Now don't chicken out," she told herself.

Without making a sound, she crept out of bed and got dressed. When the clock struck midnight she held her breath and tip toed past her parent's bedroom. Letting her breath out, she snuck down the stairs to the living room. When she reached the front door she grasped the cold hard knob and hesitated before turning it. She had no idea what noise it might make. Closing her eyes she pulled the door open, and much to her surprise, it did not make a sound. Jacy was right. No one knew she was leaving the house.

Stepping outside she carefully closed the door. The evening air felt fresh on her face and above her a blanket of stars covered the sky. Even though the most difficult part was over, Jenny trembled. As she carefully maneuvered the front porch steps she noticed car lights blinking across the street. A door opened and Jacy stepped out. He waved to her and she ran – literally throwing herself into his arms. She needed him to make her feel safe again.

"Look at me!" She said enthusiastically. "I'm out here and they're still sleeping! Can you believe it?"

Her fear and anxiety was quickly replaced with the excitement of the moment. Jacy hugged her and kissed her softly.

"Come on," he urged helping her into the car. "You haven't seen anything yet."

As they drove the radio blared, and out of tune voices tried to sing along. Of course, it was all in fun – they laughed at each other and themselves. Jenny glanced out the dark side window and noticed the blurry shapes of buildings whizzing by. She rolled down her window and could not help noticing how still and quiet everything seemed, except for the odd pedestrian along the sidewalk.

When they arrived at their destination, Jenny was somewhat confused. The place appeared to be just like any other building – not a house or apartment where they could party. When Jacy knocked on the front door it slowly creaked open and they were led down a long dark hallway. At the end was another door. A bouncer opened it to reveal loud music and flashing strobe lights. Once inside, the teenagers huddled together. Smoke hung stale in the air with lights of red and green coming from the ceiling. Couches lined one side of the room where couples were making out. On the other side there was a dance floor and a crowd of people rushed to make their way toward it. Jenny thought how eerie it was that with the flashing lights everyone seemed to move in slow motion.

At the same time, the excitement was palpable. Even though no one could talk over the blasting music, it didn't seem to matter. As she and Jacy moved with the crowd he held her hand tightly. She spotted Susan pop some small pills into her mouth and start dancing. Gary pulled out a joint, lit it and shared it with them. A couple of fellows chased some girls through the crowd knocking into people. Everyone else seemed to be laughing and hanging on to each other, kissing and hugging. Jenny noticed that the smell of cigarettes and grass did not mix well together and for a moment her stomach churned.

"Want to dance?" Jacy shouted, but the music was too loud. All Jenny could do was smile as she watched him mouth the words. Scanning the room, she saw Sandy in a corner with a fellow hanging onto her nibbling her neck.

"Do you want to dance?" Jacy hollered again, this time holding her face with his hands and his mouth touching her ear.

Goose bumps raced down her back. "Sure," she replied.

On the dance floor their bodies moved to the music. Every now and then someone bumped them and they lost their balance. The strobe lights made Jenny dizzy but even that seemed exciting. When a slow song came on Jacy held her close and she could barely breathe. As she followed his steps she thought she might faint but he clung to her tightly. He moved his head close to hers and sucked in the sweet aroma of her hair. Jacy let his cheek touch hers and as electricity ran through her, his lips found hers. He gripped the back of her shirt while she ran her fingers through his long dark hair. Hot and short of breath, Jenny thought she must be in love. However, Jacy knew better. It was the grass and the atmosphere that turned her on so much.

At about 4 a.m., Jacy decided it was time to leave. He found Amanda and Sandy dancing and they helped look for Susan and Gary. Susan was passed out on a couch and Gary was as high as a kite. With everyone else's help, they made it out to the car. On the way back home, the radio was off and no one talked. In the quiet stillness Jacy held Jenny close and every so often, they shared a passionate kiss. When they reached her street Jacy turned to look directly into her eyes.

"See you Monday," he said kissing her hard one last time.

Jenny left the car smiling but when she raised her eyes to see her house across the street, the nervousness rushed back. She had to sneak back in again and the thought of it frightened her. Slowly and carefully she mounted the porch steps. She could feel her heart beat faster, and her breathing became short and quick. She knew her hair and clothes reeked of cigarettes and grass. If she were caught like that, the jig would be up.

"Relax," she told herself. "You can do it."

Almost numb with fear, she grabbed the doorknob and carefully turned it. Before entering she hesitated. The house was so dark and still that it almost psyched her out. If someone jumps out at me, I'll have a heart attack, she thought.

She knew no one was awake but that did not allay her fears. Forgetting she'd held her breath, she suddenly let it go in a gush of air and immediately covered her mouth. Despite her trepidation, she managed to make it to her room and breathed a sigh of relief as she fell onto her bed. She had a terrific time with her friends and wanted to stay awake to revel in it but knew sleep would be her greatest friend. Morning would come early.

13. Sneaking Out

When March rolled around, Kristina arrived home with the heart wrenching news of a senior who tried to beat the train but did not make it and was killed. She explained that he'd gone to the mall for lunch with some friends. They went in two cars but he decided to stay a little longer than the rest so he drove back alone. Time got away from him and with only ten minutes before the bell would ring, he dashed down the street even before the railroad lights went on. Checking the distance of the train to him, he knew he would be late if he were forced to wait for it to go by. Then he made the fatal decision to hit the gas pedal to speed up even more. He glanced to the left and saw the train coming closer but thought for sure that his car could outrun it. He heard the train's horn sound a warning but ignored it and kept on going. It was a deadly decision. The train hit the brakes but due to its speed could not stop fast enough. His car sped half way over the tracks before the train hit the driver's side head on. The poor fellow was thrown right through the windshield.

The school hallways echoed with crying and mourning that afternoon, and into the rest of the week. On Friday the students were given time off to attend his funeral. The teen's mother was so enraged by the loss of her son that she later began picketing the school grounds. Each day she carried a poster of her son with the words 'Stop Open

Campus,' which meant she did not want the students to be allowed to leave the school during lunchtime. The risk was just too great. She walked around the property several times and it did not take long before other mothers stood with her supporting her cause. They knew it could just as easily have been one of their children who crossed paths with that train. And to Kristina's surprise, their mother joined them on her day off.

§

During March and April Jenny lived a double life. During the day she attended school and went to church on Sundays. She helped her mother with housework, assisted her brother with his homework and still fought with her siblings, like those in most families. But late on Friday nights she snuck out to take in a completely different world - one filled with excitement, dances, raves and drugs. She lived for the here and now, with no thought of tomorrow or the possible consequences. She assumed everything was fine until one Saturday morning when she awoke to see her mother standing at her bedroom door. They needed to talk, she said.

"Get up young lady," Marie demanded in an authoritative tone.

Jenny glanced at the clock and realized it was already noon.

"Hurry up and get dressed. I'll meet you in the kitchen."

Jenny was taken aback by her tone but quickly dismissed it. She washed her face, brushed her teeth and donned her clothes. When she finally strolled into the kitchen, she headed right to the refrigerator.

"What's up?" She asked nonchalantly.

She poured herself a glass of orange juice and put some bread in the toaster. All the while, Marie stared at her intently. After she made some toast, she sat down at the kitchen table.

"Where did you go last night?" Marie asked catching her off guard. She knew her daughter had changed since the family moved. She seemed to have aged, especially over the past few months... and not in a good way. There were bags under her eyes and her skin looked sallow. She had also lost some weight. Marie was not at all pleased and wanted to know why.

I wonder just how much she knows? Jenny thought sitting frozen in her chair. Finally her body moved allowing her to spread some peanut butter on her toast.

"What are you talking about?" She asked innocently.

Marie tilted her head to one side. Surely Jenny did not think she was that stupid. She resisted the urge to grab her shoulders and shake some sense into her. Instead opting to remain calm, and wait for her daughter to explain her behavior. Jenny could feel her mother's eyes boring into her.

"Well?" She asked, as if she were the questioner rather than her mother. Marie flashed back to their life in Indiana when her daughter spent time with Ashley and books. So much had changed and she seemed to barely know her daughter anymore.

"I really don't know what you're talking about," Jenny added, her heart pounding. She dropped her half-eaten toast on her plate having suddenly lost her appetite. Then her throat felt as if it were closing up making it hard to swallow. She could feel her hands perspiring so she put them under the table and wiped them on her pants.

"I heard something last night," Marie said.

"What do you mean?"

"A noise… and I really wasn't sure what I heard, but when I went to your bedroom, you weren't there. So where did you go?"

"A party," she replied squirming in her seat. "That's all."

Jenny had never felt so uncomfortable – or guilty, and feared her mother would see through her lies. But even if she did, who was she to get in the way of her fun? It was her life, and her time to experiment and learn new things. She longed for Fridays and to be with Jacy. They smoked some grass and got a little high – no big deal. They smoked and danced, and then later ended up on one of the couches making out. She loved the way his hands caressed her body as he kissed her sending goose bumps all over her. She did not understand how or why her body tingled so much, or why her hips longed to be next to his, but she sure was enjoying the ride and did not want it to end.

"Whose party?" Marie demanded her arms across her chest, and her legs crossed at the knees. She looked like a commander reprimanding one of her troop.

Jenny knew she had to think fast. She'd become addicted to Jacy, and to all the new and exciting things she experienced.

"Mom, just someone at school," she said looking at her mother with frantic eyes. "Their parents were out of town and the whole school showed up."

"How dare you leave this house without us knowing when and where you're going!" Marie said glaring at her daughter. "You're grounded young lady!"

Marie envisioned a raucous event with kids dancing, drinking and throwing toilet paper all over tree branches outside. Calming herself, she continued.

"You are to be home right after school and there will be no friends or phone calls for a month." She hoped that punishment would change Jenny's ways and make her more responsible. "You understand, right?"

Jenny got up and dragged herself from the table.

"Yes, ma'am," she said turning on her heels and leaving the kitchen.

She was terrified to tell Jacy at school on Monday but knew she must. She added that she was now being watched, but he only laughed and told her not to worry. He'd find a way to get her out, he said. Then his touch and kiss gave her the reassurance she so desperately needed.

Jacy could always find a solution to her problems. He showed her how to take a screen off a window and by doing so, how she would have different areas within the house where she could get in and out. They also decided to change the nights that they met so no one would be any wiser when she did sneak out.

Jacy seemed to enjoy the ups and downs of this tumultuous ride with Jenny. After all, she was hot, naïve and a virgin to boot. Everything seemed so new to her and he enjoyed being the one to teach her new things. He loved how sensual she got when she smoked weed and how her body reacted to his touch. He was not new to deceit and doing whatever it took to be with the person he wanted, even if there was a roadblock: parents. And Jenny's folks simply offered a new challenge.

Having Sandy befriend her in the first place was his idea and it worked like a charm. She was his flavor of the year and he knew how to be convincing when necessary. Plus he knew she loved him, which made it all that much easier. He only needed patience while he introduced her to cigarettes, grass, booze, drugs, and music, but the reward was well worth the effort. The only problem was that he found himself falling in love. That was not in his plan, but there was just something about her. Not just her innocence, but also her way of showing kindness to others, even strangers. In fact even when he acted rudely toward people she still exhibited her sensitive side toward them.

14. The Final Temptation

Marie kept busy with other mothers protesting to keep their children safe on the school grounds during lunchtime. Kristina and some of the other students noticed the signs being flagged in an arc around the front of the school. Finally the principal called a meeting with the mothers and the students. He planned an assembly on a cool May morning.

The principal advised the parents that the cafeteria was not equipped to handle all of the students at one time. Separate lunchtimes would have to be scheduled, and the school would need to hire more food vendors to take care of them as well. He noted that although he understood their concern about leaving the campus, he felt the number of students actually injured or killed was minimal. Many of the students wanted to leave and eat elsewhere so they clapped when he said this. They would soon be in college and preferred to be treated like adults. However, the parents were outraged and several arguments broke out between parents and students.

"How many kids have to die?" Shouted the mother of the last boy who died. Her voice shrieked loudly making everyone turn and stare. As the audience settled down, the women shouted again – this time in unison. "How many children have to die?"

A woman in a black dress, hat and veil covering her face seemed to lead the throng of angry mothers. It was Mrs. Everstein whose son Stephen also died while returning late to school. Like the others, he tried to beat the train. Although she could not blame the school for her son's tardiness or his decision to race the train, he did die because of it and she hoped adding her voice would help stop it from happening to anyone in the future.

"My son is dead!" She yelled.

Silence hung heavy in the air as the word DEAD seemed to come alive. As she brushed stray tears from her cheeks, she repeated the words.

"He is dead. Do you understand? D E A D," she spelled out. "He will never attend school again, never go to his prom, never graduate, never marry or have children."

No longer able to control her tears, she gasped for breath. Amongst faint whispers, a few other mothers could be heard muffling their cries. Some women held babies close to their chests – undoubtedly fearing for their own children's lives one day.

"How many more lives will be lost before you take a stand and realize that this is a dangerous situation?" She asked, her body trembling. "We can't change the fact that the railroad is just a couple of blocks away and the students have to cross the tracks to go and eat. It is when they return in a hurry to the school that they risk their lives," she added tearfully. "But we can change the degree of control we have over our children's safety. If they can't leave the school, they can't get hurt."

As the parents clapped, her husband put his arms around her and they slowly walked toward the exit door.

Then the noise became unbearable. Many people attempted to state their opinions at once. Finally the principal, who could see that the meeting was getting out of control, took his kerchief from his pocket and wiped perspiration from his forehead. He felt terrible about the deaths that had occurred but at the same time, he had to do his job. He realized that making the necessary changes would not happen overnight.

"First," he said sincerely as he watched the couple leave the auditorium, "I want to say how sorry I am for the loss of your son."

The Eversteins walked out and did not even acknowledge him. As he stood before the other parents, he felt his pulse quicken and a hot flash overcame him. He knew he'd have to come up with something or he might have a riot on his hands. Meanwhile, the parents grew more enraged and raised their voices even louder.

"Second," the principal shouted this time, "I will put all of this under advisement and will get my staff together immediately to talk about this serious problem. This issue will not be ignored," he asserted and added flatly, "This meeting is adjourned until further notice."

As he slowly walked off the stage he could hear the chide remarks of the parents along with the protests of the students, and knew the issue was far from over.

§

The month of May brought sprouting tulips and other colorful flowers, as well as greening buds on the trees. The sun shone brightly with the promise of warmer weather even though the thermometer still showed sixty degrees. Jenny tried to be extra careful. She did not want to get caught sneaking out again. Following Jacy's instructions, she removed the screen from the living room window and hid it in the bushes the day before her planned escape. Other times, she exited via the front or back doors. She made sure her chores were completed each day so her mother would have nothing to be suspicious about. However, there were some nights that her mother checked up on her making it too difficult to leave.

Marie made arrangements for Jenny to attend a church retreat on the last weekend in May. She was still going to church but not as active as she use to be. The plan involved meeting organizers at the church and Jenny staying at a host home for the weekend. While there, she would carry out some community service and attend prayer meetings. There were also such events as campfires where they could roast marshmallows and talk about God.

Marie's plan was two-fold. Not only would she get Jenny away from the crowd she'd been hanging out with for a while, but she might also draw closer to God – always a good thing in her eyes. It pleased Marie to see Jenny so willing to do what she asked, but unbeknownst to her mother, she had other plans. She excitedly packed her bag for the trip making sure to include everything on her list from the church: slacks, shirts, underwear, socks, flashlight and a Bible. To Marie, she seemed excited about leaving for the weekend. When Jenny entered the kitchen with suitcase in hand Marie asked, "Ready to go?"

"I still have to get my sleeping bag and pillow," she replied and ran to the garage to fetch them.

Marie laughed under her breath as she watched her daughter eagerly put all her stuff together. She felt such extreme happiness over the fact that Jenny looked forward to the church retreat. This was the daughter she knew and remembered. Marie walked over to her suitcase and picked it up as she re-entered the kitchen.

Maybe this will do her some good after all, she thought.

As Jenny followed her mother to the car she kept her secret emotions under control. She stood holding her sleeping bag and pillow while Marie opened the back door and carefully placed the suitcase inside. Then Jenny tossed in the other items.

"Anything else you need?" Marie asked before shutting the door.

"Nope," she replied giving her mom a big hug. As she slid in the front seat she added, "Thanks mom. I've got everything now."

"Well, if you need anything else don't hesitate to call," Marie said as she drove to the church. Jenny sat with a huge smile on her face. She could not believe how her emotions played with her and how difficult it was to keep her composure.

"So do you have any idea what you guys are going to be doing?" Marie asked.

"I think we're going into some neighborhoods to help clean them up."

"Sounds like fun."

"No, it doesn't Mom," Jenny replied rolling her eyes, "...but we have to treat our neighbors as we want to be treated and lend a helping hand."

Boy did she have that response down pat! Marie leaned over and patted her daughter's leg. "I'm so proud of you for volunteering."

Her mother's praise made Jenny feel uncomfortable. In fact she did not even want to talk about the church retreat. Fortunately for her, Marie drove the rest of the way in silence, but happy inside that her daughter was being so agreeable. When they arrived, Marie helped her daughter get her things out of the car.

"Mom, I can get them," Jenny insisted and leaned over to give her mother a kiss. Then she picked everything up - sort of - doing a balancing act to show her mother that she could do it herself. Marie shrugged and waved goodbye as she drove off. Jenny moved her belongings to the side of the building before she put them down. After about fifteen minutes, a car drove up. Amanda and Jacy got out, and helped her put her stuff inside.

"Ready for a fun weekend?" Jacy asked as they drove off.

Jenny grinned widely and cuddled close to him. He embraced her and gently kissed her on the lips. She placed her head on his shoulder and relaxed – knowing they would spend the weekend together.

They drove for some time before Jenny noticed primarily farmland all around them. The radio was on and Jacy puffed on a cigarette, flicking ashes out the side window. Finally they pulled up to a small cottage in the middle of a thick patch of trees.

"Where are we?" She asked. "It's so beautiful here."

"Thanks," Amanda replied. "It's all right, I guess. This is my family's vacation home."

Amanda's parents were out of state for the weekend, and gave her permission to invite some friends as long as they behaved. Jenny could not believe the freedom her friend was allowed. Her own mother would never let her have friends over without adult supervision.

From the car window she could see a long house with an attached three-car garage. When they walked around back, a little past the property, she found a pond stocked with fish.

"Gonna have a party tonight!" Amanda exclaimed, her arms animated and waving over her head clapping. "I can't wait. I actually have a DJ coming and a couple of kegs of beer. This is our end of school year and beginning of summer party!"

Inside the house, the foyer was charming with ceramic tile and a mirror with a gold frame around it. As they walked straight ahead to the living room they could see that it was decorated in various shades of blue. To the right was the kitchen with glass patio doors leading out to an over-sized porch. From there they could see the horizon.

"What a beautiful view," Jenny noted.

As they walked down a hallway Amada gladly displayed her bedroom before showing her guests where they would sleep. She would share her room with Susan, while Sandy and Gary would bunk together.

"...and this is your room," she said to Jenny and Jacy.

A sneaky smile crossed her face and Jenny could not help blushing. When Amanda turned to leave, Jenny moved closer to Jacy and whispered in his ear.

"I think she's mistaken?"

"Mistaken about what?" He asked with a slight grin.

He already knew how many bedrooms there were and that they would share one together. In fact, he helped her with the sleeping arrangements.

"She forgot to give you a room," Jenny said nervously but he just laughed. "Can't you share a room with Gary, and I share a room with Susan?" She suggested.

"She didn't make any mistakes," he said confidently.

"We're sharing this room?" She asked innocently. She stood in the doorway, her eyes opened wide and her body stiff as a statue.

Jacy moved close and caressed her shoulders. Then he whispered, "It will be all right. We're in love aren't we?"

He took the bags from her hands and placed them on the floor by the bed, but Jenny did not budge. Jacy walked back and put her hands in his. Lifting them to his face, he gently kissed each knuckle without looking up. When he kissed her neck, the hair on her arms stood up and he grinned with delight. Silently, he closed the door. With little kisses around her neck to her cheeks and then to her mouth, he slowly got her to move toward the bed. She took little baby steps until finally it was right besides her.

Throwing caution to the wind, Jenny let her emotions control her actions. Her breath quickened while her heart pounded hard and fast. His lips found hers again and molded into a deep kiss. He carefully leaned her onto the bed and knelt over her. His hands caressed her shoulders and arms slowly moving to her chest. He began kissing her hard and his pelvis went down on top of her moving in little circles. She gasped for air as she let her fingers stroke his hair and she drew him closer. He went for her throat and she moaned delighting in the touch of his kisses on her skin. Then there was a knock at the bedroom door.

"What is it?" Jacy asked out of breath.

"We have things to do before the party tonight, Jacy," Amanda said with a giggle.

He rolled onto his side leaving Jenny struggling for air.

"Fine," Jacy shouted somewhat perturbed. "Give us a minute."

They lied on the bed for a few seconds holding hands so they could calm down and regain their composure.

"We'll finish this later," Jacy said kissing her softly.

Amanda had lots of food for sandwiches, as well as chips and dips, and cokes and beer. When the party began the house filled of people dancing, drinking, and smoking grass. Jenny took a couple of drags, which put her in a happy and relaxed mood.

"Try this," Jacy suggested, offering her a pill with her coke.

Nervously, she shook her head. She was not so sure she wanted to actually try any kind of pills. Weed was one thing, and it already made her feel romantic, but she had heard of people overdosing with pills. She did not want to be one of them.

"Come on," Jacy coaxed with soft baby kisses on her neck. He knew her soft spot and how to get her excited. He blew gently into her ear, which gave her a rush of emotion over her entire body.

"Please, with me?" He urged holding her close and lifting her chin to look into his dark pleading eyes. "I don't want to do this alone."

Jenny still hesitated. The thought of pills actually scared her despite Jacy's words. Then he let the big 'L' word drop as his eyes pierced into hers. "I love you, Jenny," he said.

She longed to hear those words and he knew it. She got lost in his gaze and let him put the pill in her mouth. She took a drink and swallowed it. Everyone drank and laughed, bumping into her while dancing to the loud music. After about twenty minutes, the room began to swirl in circles, while the cigarette smoke choked her. She could not stand still.

"Are you all right?" Jacy asked grabbing her when she

almost fell.

Jenny just smiled at him adoringly.

"I love you," she said throwing her arms around him.

She kissed his neck and then his cheek until she found his mouth. Of course, Jacy responded to each move. He picked her up and carried her down the hall to their room. He laid her gently on the bed and kissed her hard again. She was high and out of control, and he intended to take advantage of it.

"I love you too," he whispered.

He watched her squirm with the excitement of his breath on her body. He molded his lips onto hers and his tongue gently forced her mouth open wider. He found her body exciting to touch; he let his fingers graze the top of her shoulders as he kissed her neck. She accepted every move and even though he knew it was the drugs that were making her so amenable, he did not care. He wanted her – all of her.

He slowly unbuttoned her blouse and his excitement rose as he looked at her. He nibbled his way down from her mouth to her neck and then on to her breasts. She moaned as they kissed passionately, her body moving with a slow, rhythmic movement. He kissed his way to her belly and unsnapped her pants. Lifting up her hips, he pulled them down. She panted hard, not fully understanding but trusting him completely.

"You know how much I love you," he whispered caressing her legs. Jenny could only sigh blissfully in response. She never felt like this before and did not want it to stop.

"Tell me you know it," he insisted.

"Yes," she whispered.

"Tell me you want me to make love to you."

He gently massaged her thighs and her body tingled with excitement. She could not control her emotions or even begin to comprehend what was happening.

"Tell me it's all right to love you," he whispered kissing her supple lips.

She shivered and panted as he continued to explore her body.

"Tell me," he urged in between hot kisses.

Her head told her no but the drugs had taken control.

All she could muster was a weak "yes," prompting Jacy to hop up, shed his own clothes and let them drop to the floor. Jenny had never seen a naked boy before and for a split second the sight frightened her. He climbed back onto the bed, his body covering hers. His skin felt warm and moist against hers. He kissed her again moving slowly to her neck. She kissed his cheek tasting his salty skin. His body so close to hers - skin on skin - moving slowly up and down was so arousing. Then he thrust his pelvis into hers.

"Ow!" She cried, as he pushed forcefully into her.

His body damp and shaking, he held tightly onto her arms but she tried to push him away. He knew it always hurt the first time but he was determined to have her.

"Sorry," he managed to whisper, as he slowly moved in and out, up and down, until he was satisfied.

Finally he gasped aloud, found her mouth and kissed her again. When he let her go, he fell on his side still holding her. He knew he had one more night with her so he tried to be gentle. With any luck, he might get to do her a second time. Still in an embrace, they fell asleep.

15. The Scare

As usual the family gathered around the television on Friday nights. On this particular night, Erik, Jessica and Regina wanted to watch Jurassic Park. The evening began with laughing and screaming when the dinosaurs went on a rampage. Then the phone rang, which launched Marie from the couch. After listening for a moment her voice trembled so Jim rushed to her side.

"Is something wrong?" He asked.

"It's Pastor Clem and he wants to know why Jenny isn't at the retreat. I dropped her off right in front of the church. How could this be?"

She seemed so excited about going on the retreat Marie thought, and tried to recall their conversation that day.

She remembered that Jenny took everything out of the car herself and kissed her on the cheek before she left. Her heart skipped a beat and she could not think straight. Jim suggested that they go to their bedroom to talk so the children could finish watching the movie.

"Where do you think she is?" Marie asked, her imagination running wild. Her question was mixed with hope and skepticism as she paced the floor. She spoke softly so as not to alarm the rest of her family, but inside she was a jumble of nerves and her stomach a ball of knots. She was not sure how she was supposed to feel, but a sense of helpless and dread consumed her. At the same time, she was angry that her daughter might have deceived her. Jim held her close and tried to console her.

"Honey, I'm sure she is fine," he soothed. He felt the tenseness of her body as her tears gushed out.

"How could she do this to us?" She sobbed.

"She isn't thinking straight, honey," he said holding her tighter. Jim's face burned red with anger. He could not stand to see his wife so distraught.

"What if she's hurt or something? She could be lying in a ditch somewhere. Maybe she's dead!" Her imagination finally won out.

"Don't think such awful things, Marie," Jim suggested. "I think she had this planned all along."

Jim held her gently, but his hands formed fists behind her back. He had to remain calm if he wanted his wife to relax. Taking a deep breath, he closed his eyes and tried to relax. Marie slipped from his arms and headed for the bathroom. As she passed the mirror she saw her reflection and felt as if she had aged ten years in just a few minutes. Mascara creased her cheeks leaving a black trail of tears. Picking up a cloth, she washed her face.

"You might be right Jim," she said thinking back. "She was in an awfully good mood when I dropped her off." She wondered if Jenny had left any clues as to where she might really be.

"What did the pastor say?" Asked Jim, frowning.

"He advised us not say anything to her when we pick her up at the church on Sunday. He said to wait so he could confront her on Monday. He intends to ask her why she did this." Her body shook as she sat down on the bed.

"What if she's hurt, Jim?" She cried. "What if he's wrong, and we don't look for her, and she doesn't show up at the church?"

"What if he's right," Jim asked. "Do you think you can do as he asked?" He knelt down in front of her, took her hands in his and searched her face. Another stream of tears slipped down Marie's cheeks.

"I don't know."

"Well, you should, Marie. The pastor knows what he's doing. He's most likely right and she probably won't lie to him."

Marie glanced up at her husband with sad eyes and he wiped the teardrops from her face.

"How do I not ask her where she's been?"

"It's called tough love, Marie."

She realized he was right but wondered how she could wait a full day to find out where her daughter really went. She finally decided to dry her tears and apply some makeup so she could put on an act in front of the kids. As far as they knew everything was fine, and she wanted to keep it that way.

To Marie, the weekend seemed like the longest in history. With too much time on her hands, her mind was overwhelmed with dreadful thoughts and her heart filled with fear over the possible plight of her daughter. Sunday could not arrive fast enough.

To her surprise, Jenny showed up at the church in time for the service and acted as if the retreat was terrific. She was totally animated as she related how they cleaned up a city block and what a great time she had at the campfire.

Is this what happens when kids become teenagers? Marie wondered. *They test their parents and lie to them?* The pastor was obviously right.

Marie recalled the first time her oldest daughter Kristina had an overnight guest. They quietly watched television and ate popcorn. Afterward Marie showed the girls how to jump on the bed and have a pillow fight. Then she got out the nail polish and helped them paint their nails.

So how did this happen with Jenny? She wondered. Jenny was the complete opposite and a proficient liar as well. There was nothing Marie could say or do at that point, because the pastor would be taking matters into his own hands.

On Monday morning Marie woke the kids for school and was happy to be back into a routine. That day, Jenny and Jacy met for lunch as usual. However this time, they talked of how she fooled her parents and the amazing weekend they shared together. After being so close and making love, Jenny truly believed Jacy was the one and *only* one for her. He had told her that he loved her and her heart leapt with joy.

After school Marie surprised her by picking her up.

"Come on," she beckoned with a fake smile.

Jacy watched curiously as Jenny got into her mother's car instead of Amanda's. She glanced back at him with a terrified look.

"Where are we going?" She asked.

Marie felt her breath catch in her throat and did not answer. She wondered if she could really pull this off and do what the preacher asked. Switching on the radio to her oldies station, she began to sing along. In response, Jenny switched the station to more hip music that she liked. It took only minutes to get to the church.

"Mom," she asked barely able to breathe, "...why are we going to church?"

Marie kept her eyes on the road. She wanted to cry but had to be strong.

"The pastor wants to see us," she said in a controlled voice.

Jenny turned her head toward her side window. She did not want her mother to see the fear in her eyes. Once the car was parked, they strolled toward the big front doors of the church. Jenny's stomach churned. She knew she'd been caught.

"Hello, Marie, Jenny," said Pastor Clem. He shook their hands before pointing to chairs for them to sit down. Jenny's hands began to shake so she folded them tightly together in her lap. *Could she be wrong?* She wondered. Moisture slowly bubbled across her forehead and the back of her neck.

"Thanks for seeing us today," said Marie.

"My pleasure," he replied, to reassure her with his voice. He stood straight and tall with his arms wrapped across his chest - like a judge waiting to issue a verdict.

"Jenny," he began, giving her his full attention. "How was your weekend?"

She wanted to say it was great. She wanted to lie and make up something that she did with the church group but knew it was futile. She'd been caught red handed like the kid who stole from the cookie jar. The pastor stared at her and waited for an answer as she twisted and squirmed in her chair. Then she lifted her head and looked him square in the eyes.

"It was very nice sir," she said arrogantly.

Marie could not believe what she heard and hated the fact that they were correct in their thinking. She had hoped Jenny would see the error of her ways and apologize right away.

"Do you think it was nice to worry your parents like you did?" The pastor pressed on.

Why would they worry about me? She wondered.

"What do you mean?" She asked frowning and staring

at her feet. She just could not look at him.

"Don't you think they worried about you? How would you feel if your mom told you she went someplace, and you found out that she never went there?" He took a breath to let what he said sink in before he continued. "...and she never called you to let you know if she was safe, so you had no idea where she was or even if she was alive?"

Jenny rolled her eyes at the thought and figured he was blowing everything out of proportion. Of course she was fine and if it had been the other way around, she would have thought mom was just hanging out with friends. She peeked over at her mother who cried silently into a Kleenex. The sight of her being so upset and frightened broke Jenny's heart. Her intent was to have fun, not hurt her mother.

"I think you owe her a huge apology, don't you?" The pastor asked sternly.

Jenny looked up and for the first time saw anger on his face. She wished she could get out of there – and fast. She just wanted to go home. Again her eyes drifted to her mother, who continued to fight back tears.

"I'm sorry for making you worry mom."

Marie did not look up, but gasped aloud. Tears raced down her face like a faucet as she let herself go.

"I hope you realize that there are consequences for your actions young lady," said Pastor Clem. Shifting from one foot to the other he added, "...and I don't want you to ever use one of our retreats as a lie again. Do you understand?"

"Yes sir."

The pastor ended the session with a prayer and when they left, they walked to the car in silence.

Marie blew her nose one last time before starting the

car. The silence on the way home was deafening. Jenny's head swam. She was so upset that she could not think straight. One moment she recalled her weekend with Jacy and the next she thought of her mother worrying about her. She had never considered that her parents might be worried. She actually thought they believed she was with the church group.

"Hey," Jim called to Jenny when they walked into the house.

Jenny found him standing in the kitchen staring into the refrigerator.

"Yeah?" She responded.

Marie soon joined them and stood silently by.

"Do you understand why you saw Pastor Clem?" Her father asked.

"What I don't understand is why you two couldn't tell me yesterday when you picked me up that you knew I wasn't at the retreat," she said visibly perturbed. She sat down on a kitchen chair and crossed her legs.

"Oh," Jim said closing the fridge door. "Do you think us saying something would have made as big of an impact?"

Jenny rolled her eyes shamelessly, and shook her head while Jim sat down beside her. "If you're saying would I have known that I was caught, yes. All you had to do was tell me." She really did not want to deal with her father's cross-examination. The pastor already told her she did wrong, and that she would be punished. She just wanted to hear what her punishment might be, and go to her room.

"You surprise me young lady," he added tapping his fingers on the table. "You act like this is our fault."

Jenny's eyes shot angrily up to him. Marie felt an uneasy knot in her stomach and bit her lip as she listened.

She was not sure how much more tension she could handle in one day.

"You are the ones who embarrassed me in front of the pastor," she replied impudently. Her eyes continued to pierce into Jim's like swords. In response to her words, he jerked backward, got up and paced the floor. Exasperation and outrage at her insolent response was evident in his movement.

"Don't you dare turn this around Jenny. Do you think we told the pastor that you didn't show up?"

"I don't want to talk about this anymore," she replied squeezing her eyes tightly shut. Then she stood up and put her hands on her hips.

"Young lady," he said sternly, "How do you think we found out that you weren't at the retreat?"

He felt his face grow hot, and his eyebrows moved down to the center of his nose. Marie could not help hearing the angry tone in his voice. It frightened her and in response she wrapped her arms about herself, as if giving a hug.

"I really don't know," Jenny shouted back undaunted. Her body tensed as her hands formed fists that started to shake at her sides. Slowly she moved toward the stairs hoping to put an end to the conversation once and for all.

Jim was not about to let it go. "He called us," he said with obvious outrage.

Jenny's eyes opened wide, her mouth dropped open and she stopped abruptly in her tracks.

"It was his idea to tell you himself, not ours," Jim added. "It was never our intent to embarrass you, but rather to teach you a lesson."

Jenny moved away from the stairs and slinked back down onto the kitchen chair. As she laid her head on one arm, she realized that she had it all wrong. The pastor called looking for her. *Who would have thought of that?* She wondered, staring at the floor counting the squares in the tile.

"You're due for punishment, correct?" He asked firmly.

Jenny knew that was coming. She already envisioned a summer without her friends. Drawing a deep breath she replied, "Yes."

Marie stepped away from the wall to join them at the table. Jenny did not look up as she heard the chair move and her mother clear her throat.

"Honey," Marie began, "...you know we love you, right?"

At first she did not answer but just stared at her mother. Finally she raised her head from the table.

"I know mom," she whispered.

A look of relief covered Marie's face. "You are grounded for the entire summer," she announced.

"That's not fair!" Jenny groaned slapping a hand on the table. "Maybe a week or two, but not all summer!"

Jim glared at her with a warning look. In response, she sighed aloud and rolled her eyes again.

"That's just not fair mom," she repeated, her eyes filling with tears. *This can't be happening*, she thought. *It's my worst nightmare!*

"You've been lying to us a lot lately," Marie continued. "You've been sneaking out, and I smelled cigarette smoke on some of your clothes when I did the laundry." Marie pulled up a chair and sat down beside her.

"Aside from being grounded, there will be no friends visiting and no phone calls. Only family."

Jenny hung her head as she listened and twitched

uncomfortably in her chair.

"If we didn't love you, we wouldn't punish you. We just wouldn't care."

Marie hoped Jenny would realize that the punishment was for her own good and in fact, deep down Jenny did. Jenny recalled the talk with the pastor and hearing his prayer:

Help this young lady to realize that she is your daughter and to let your love and compassion show through her. Remind her that her body is her temple. Help her realize that she is loved. Help her understand that her actions are important, and that there are consequences to decisions made and acted out. We know you love her Lord, even if she did wrong. Help her to see that, and to ask for forgiveness. Be with this family, make them strong and learn from this situation.

As the words echoed in her mind, she recognized that she had been acting like someone else by behaving so deceivingly - and she did not like who she had become. But she also thought of Jacy, and their weekend together haunted her. *Will I ever see him again?* She wondered. With the punishment doled out, Jenny rose from her chair. As she left the kitchen she heard the word: "Pray."

16. Jail Time

When Jenny awoke the following day she realized it was the first day of her jail sentence. She could faintly make out the muffled sounds of the television and it reminded her that summer vacation had arrived. Undoubtedly it would be a long one with no friends, including Jacy. It would not be too difficult to quit the cigarettes and grass since she wouldn't be hanging with her friends. She would only be able to talk with her siblings. She felt as if she were in prison- confined to the house as if it were her cell, but knew she had to make the best of it.

When Jenny left her room she heard Erik listening to Metallica in his bedroom so loud that his door shook. Regina and Jessica were still in their pajamas watching TV, and Kristina was getting ready for work. Marie and Jim had already left the house. She walked to the kitchen, grabbed a banana, poured a glass of orange juice and sat down at the table. Then Kristina rushed in to make a fast piece of toast.

"Mom said she left a list of chores for you to do today," she noted as she buttered her toast. "Please don't disappoint them."

Jenny thought she could offer a snappy come back but knew she deserved to be punished. "Where's the list?" She asked.

Kristina smiled at the nice tone of her voice. Moving a magnet off the fridge she passed the note to her.

"Hey," Kristina said before she left, "I only work four hours today. I can help you with whatever you don't finish okay?"

"Thanks," she replied, glad that Kristina was not angry with her too.

§

Soon the summer brought swimming classes for Jessica and Regina, while Erik played basketball. Twice a week they watched his games. Jenny decided to help out at the church nursery, and her parents allowed her to drive them around town so she could gain more experience before taking a test for her license. Good behavior would be rewarded they reminded her. Friday evenings stayed the same except that Jim and Marie brought the kids to a drive-in theater now and then as a special treat. Chores had to be completed, but instead of complaining, Jenny kept busy finishing out her prison time without grumbling and actually enjoyed her siblings again. After a couple of weeks she even began to like herself.

Around the third week of summer she experienced some trouble getting out of bed. When she sat up, the room started to spin. The smell of food made her nauseous and she could not eat. Thinking she had the flu, Marie made her stay in bed for a couple of days until she felt better. Of course the sickness passed and before long she was up doing her chores again.

In June and July, she did not get her period and began to worry. The memory of her last night with Jacy repeated in her mind. The pastor told her that there would be consequences for her actions. Little did she realize the truth of his words. Jenny finally summonsed the courage and told her mother.

"How late?" Marie asked.

"Just over two months," she replied adding that she did not feel well and thought she should see a doctor.

She fibbed and told her mother that she was having stomach cramps along with nausea and thought she had some kind of virus. Marie made an appointment for her and since she still did not have her driver's license, Kristina took her. Jenny was led into a room that not only looked clean but smelled like Lysol. There were pictures of pregnant ladies showing what a baby looked like at different stages of its development within the womb, a picture of a skeleton with all the bone's names on it, and another displaying the muscles of the body. She could not help noticing a bed with silver stirrups that looked very uncomfortable. Nevertheless, she jumped on the bed so the nurse could take her vitals.

"The doctor will be with you shortly," she said, walked out and closed the door. While she waited for the doctor, her tummy twisted not knowing what was wrong with her. After a few minutes a lady dressed in regular clothes entered with a stethoscope around her neck and shook her hand.

"I'm Doctor Sparks," she said with a comforting smile. "What's yours?"

"Jenny," she whispered.

"So why do I have the pleasure of seeing you today?"

"I haven't been feeling too good lately."

Dr. Sparks clutched her stethoscope, and asked her to breathe in and out slowly so she could listen to her lungs.

"Everything sounds normal," she said. "What's been the problem?"

"Well, I missed my period and I've felt quite

nauseated," she explained.

"What about tender breasts, fatigue, dizziness and perhaps going to the bathroom more often than usual?"

Jenny reluctantly shook her head. *How does she know?* She wondered.

"We usually don't give pap smears at this young age unless you've been sexually active," she said, which caused Jenny to squirm in her seat. The doctor noticed how uncomfortable she appeared and added, "Is there something you want to tell me?"

Jenny opened her mouth to speak but nothing came out.

"You don't have to worry, Jenny. Anything you tell me is confidential. I won't talk to your mother unless you ask me to do so."

She shook her head to indicate that she understood.

"All right dear. Have you been sexually active?"

"Yes," she replied in a quiet voice.

"Well, it sounds like you might be pregnant, so we need to take a urine sample to see if it comes up positive. It will take a couple of days, but I'll call you with the results."

The doctor handed her a small container and she headed for the bathroom. When she finished, she placed it on the counter.

During the next two days, she jumped every time the phone rang. Finally the fateful call from the doctor's office confirmed her worst fear. She was pregnant.

How am I going to explain this to mom? She thought. *Maybe I could take her to dinner. I'd better make it a public place so she won't yell at me.*

That evening when Marie arrived home from work, Jenny asked if the two of them could go for a ride and get a bite to eat.

"Mom, please?" She begged. "I made dinner for the kids, but I need to talk to you privately."

"Thanks honey," she replied taking out some plates to set the table. "But are you sure we can't just eat here and talk?"

Jenny pulled out some silverware and napkins, and placed them around the plates. *Desperate times call for desperate measures*, she thought. *I have to get mom away from everyone else.*

"Please," she urged again. "It's very important." Her body language and pouting face convinced Marie to take her seriously.

"Okay," she said as she began to fill the plates. "Kids, dinner's ready."

Her younger siblings complained that Jenny was allowed to eat out but they could not. As Jenny drove, she mulled over and over again in her head what she should say. *Mom, I'm pregnant. Mom, you're going to be a grandmother.* Or, *Please don't be mad; I didn't do this purposely but...*

By the time she drove into a fast food restaurant Marie was wringing her hands with worry about what her daughter might say.

"Mom," she said finally. She stared straight ahead as tears formed in her eyes.

"Yes, dear," Marie responded studying her daughter's face.

Jenny searched for the courage to say the right words. No way could she sneak this one by her mother. It had to be said.

Just do it, she told herself but, memories of Jacy flooded in. She heard the words *I love you*, before he took off his clothes. He held her tightly and her body responded to his touch. She could not seem to fight the feeling. She was not trying to punish anyone or get even with anyone. She was just a young girl in love. *I wonder if mom will understand? Well, here goes...*

"Mom, I'm pregnant," she said in a soft and apologetic tone. Her eyes were still closed and she envisioned Jacy's embrace.

"What?" Marie shrieked. In one swift motion, she raised her hand and struck Jenny's face. "You little whore. Is that what you've been up to - sleeping around?"

The reality of the situation struck hard and as tears flowed down her cheeks, Jenny covered her face where her mother hit her.

How could she even think I slept around? She wondered, stunned by her mother's violent reaction.

"No," she muffled in between sobs. "I haven't been sleeping around."

"Do you even know who the father is?" Marie asked sarcastically. Her imagination racing, she figured her daughter was with a number of different boys. *I did not raise her to act that way. How could she do that?*

"Yes mother," Jenny cut into her thoughts, "...as a matter of fact, I do. It's Jacy, of course. I love him," she said shaking.

A tense silence filled the car as Marie tried to take in the news. Finally everything came together and made sense. Jenny was with Jacy that weekend when she skipped the church retreat. However, Marie still saw innocence in her daughter, and her anger began to fade. She was only 16 and in love. It had been years since Marie was that age, but she tried to put herself in Jenny's shoes. Yes, she had sex and is pregnant, but it's now my job to help her get her through it.

Marie closed her eyes and took in a deep breath to regain her composure. When she opened them she saw the terror on her daughter's face, and her eyes were puffy and red. Then she felt ashamed for her reaction and her terrible thoughts.

"Jenny," Marie said raising a hand toward her. When she flinched she added, "No, no, honey," and cupped her daughter's face in her hands. "I'm so sorry that I hit you," she whispered.

She brought Jenny's face toward her and kissed her on the forehead.

"I'm so sorry mom," she cried. "I'm so sorry."

Marie wrapped her arms around her, and rocked her back and forth. "Are you sure?" Marie asked.

The images of that night surged back into Jenny's mind, but this time she felt nauseated.

"Yes, mom," she replied. "I'm sure that I'm pregnant, and yes, Jacy is the father. I only made love with him once on the weekend you thought I was at the retreat."

Mother and daughter cried together for several moments.

"Don't cry," said Marie wiping tears from her daughter's face. "It's done. Now the hardest part comes. We have to tell your dad, but don't worry, everything will be fine."

17. The Best Laid Plans

Jacy spent the summer on the reservation with his father and enjoyed the company of the other Indians, raising crops, fishing, smoking, and getting high with the elders. Even though he could not see Jenny until school began, he thought his plan had worked just fine. When he was around her parents, he acted politely. He always asked if she could go out and when she did, he taught her to smoke cigarettes and pot, as well as drink. It was thrilling for him to see her at lunch every afternoon - that tight little body - letting her buy him his fries. Yes, he sure enjoyed the thrill of the catch.

He loved how he made her blush whenever he convinced her to do something wrong. He remembered that first time at McDonald's when he kissed her and she gasped for breath. He loved being in control and because he felt no guilt, it was easy for him to do whatever he wished anytime he wanted. He also loved how romantic she became with a little grass, but the biggest thrill of all was when he talked her into going away with him for the weekend. It took some convincing, but he thought the reward was well worth it.

His heart fluttered when he recalled how she lied to her parents so she could go with him, and the look on her face was priceless when she discovered that they would share a room. Then afterward when he gave her the Ecstasy she felt so good and they made love. He could tell she was a virgin. He remembered the satisfaction he felt as he caressed her body and she trembled with pleasure. He knew she was under his power, loving him and not wanting to let him down. Despite his deceitful plan, he was surprised to find that he missed her that summer. She had become such a huge part of his life. He felt he needed her more than ever, but did not understand why.

§

The summer passed quickly and before Jenny knew it, school began again. Since she was in a higher grade, she attended the other building and was the new kid on the block again. However, she felt as if she had aged after all she had been through. Since she was grounded all summer, she had not heard from Sandy, Susan or Amanda. Although she missed them, it did not really bother her, but she wondered why she did not hear from Jacy. She had so much to tell him.

She stood in the doorway of the new school looking at the other students coming inside. She did not want to think about her personal problems, but found herself continually replaying in her mind what happened the previous year. She could hardly remember the girl she used to be when she first arrived to Oklahoma – so fresh and innocent. *Who am I?* She wondered shaking her head. *What's going to happen to me now?* She had to find Jacy. Perhaps he had the key to the answer.

In her third-hour class she spotted the outline of his face and his long black hair tied in a ponytail. He sat up front a few seats and did not see her come in. An anxious feeling crept over her as she crossed her legs swinging her loose leg. She sucked in a deep breath and tried to make sense of this uneasy encounter. She was going to have his baby and he did not even know it. *Would he be a part of their lives, or should she prepare to live with her mom forever?* For an instant, she flashed on an image of herself standing next to him with their baby. For the first time she thought about the future so directly. She knew she was really not ready to be a mother, but what choice did she have?

When the bell rang, she froze in her seat. She stared at Jacy and willed him to look up at her. He got up and started down the row when he suddenly noticed her and his amazement registered openly on his face.

"Hi!" He said smiling. His dark eyes twinkled as he searched her face. He was clearly happy to bump into her and enjoyed seeing her blush again.

"Hey," Jenny replied attempting to sound nonchalant. She thought his gaze might melt her on the spot. Rising to gather her books, she noticed that her heart raced just like it used to do.

"How are you?" He asked as they walked together down the school hallway.

"Good," she responded shrugging her shoulders. "And you?"

They walked side-by-side - close but not touching - until she reached her next class.

"Got to go," he said kissing her quickly on the cheek. "See you after school? I'll be at the front doors."

Jenny's face immediately lit up like a Christmas tree.

"Yes!" She said, and her eyes followed him as he ran down the hall. She knew that somehow she must gather all her courage. They very much needed to talk. The day seemed to drag on as she waited for the final bell to ring.

When she found Jacy he was leaning against the entrance door waiting for her just as he promised. As they walked outside Jenny felt those old butterflies fluttering in her tummy reminding her how strongly she felt about him.

"Want a ride home?" He asked.

"Sure," she replied without thinking. She followed him to the parking lot to an old red Ford.

"Is this your truck?" She asked.

Jacy grinned and nodded as he opened the passenger side for her. He started the engine and played with the radio until he found a station he liked. As they drove off he said, "I hope you don't have to be home right away. Do you want to park?"

When she smiled in the affirmative, he offered a somewhat evil grin. He figured he still had it and she would continue to do his bidding. The familiar streets soon turned into thousands of trees and he looked for a secluded area where he could pull in. He followed a paved road until he found a spot away from everyone and everything else. Finally he shut off the truck and turned to her. They were alone - totally alone. He reached out to touch her, but she had already pushed the car door open and was getting out.

"Where are you going?" Jacy asked startled. He reached over and tried to grab her blouse to pull her back in. It seemed he hoped she would be the flavor of the year one more time.

"Can we take a little walk?" She asked turning to look at him.

Jacy locked the truck and they followed a path into the forest. It was quiet at first as the wind moved gently through the trees and the leaves rustled with a swishing sound around them. He finally got the courage to take her hand and she gladly gave it. Then she realized how much she missed that simple gesture of affection.

"Did you have a good summer?" He asked gliding his fingers into the middle of hers.

"Not too bad," she said, knowing so much more must be said.

As they walked over the uneven ground, Jenny tripped over a broken branch lying in front of her path. Thinking quickly, Jacy caught her up into his arms. His breath quickened and he leaned close to her. He let his fingers trace her face from her cheek to her chin. Her heart began pounding as she leaned back bracing herself on a tree. His face lowered onto hers and their lips met in a deep kiss. When he let her loose, she panted for air. Stepping aside, she realized that she just could not do this again. This is what got her into trouble in the first place. However, Jacy was in no mood to quit. He fumbled with her blouse as he slid his hand down her chest, but she pushed him away.

"No!" She shouted.

Jacy ignored her and leaned his body closer to hers - so tight that he could feel her body shaking next to his. He slipped his hand under her shirt and moved it upward from her waist.

"Stop it, Jacy!" She hollered with tears in her eyes, but he was so strong that she could not push him away. Finally with all the strength she could muster, she lifted her knee and jammed it into his groin.

"Ow!" He screamed, and dropped to the ground holding his crotch.

"What did you do that for?" He asked in short choppy words. His eyes scanned her face as tears streamed down her cheeks.

"I don't understand, Jenny. Why are you crying? I'm the one in pain."

Jenny turned and ran toward the truck, and he limped along behind her. When she reached it she crossed her arms in front of her and waited for him.

"I want to go home," she announced.

"Why are you such a tease?" He asked angrily. Deep down this act of playing hard to get actually turned him on.

"I am not a tease, Jacy. I just want to go home now."

He walked around her dangling his keys in front of her face.

"Not until I get what I came here for," he laughed with an evil hiss. "You know you want it."

He continued circling her, studying her body while the wind pressed her clothes showing her curves. Jenny did not know what to do. She did not intend to have sex with Jacy. She just wanted to talk to him – to let him know that he was about to become a father. But after seeing his heartless behavior, she was not so sure that she wanted him to be the father of her child. She moved toward a curb and sat down. Jacy limped over and slumped down beside her.

"Jacy," she said softly looking him straight into the eyes. "It's important that we talk." Jenny recalled the night she lost her virginity. It was the only time she had sex and she got pregnant. Talk about rotten odds! She wondered how Sandy could do it so many times and it never happened to her. *Life just isn't fair!* She thought, and then drew in a deep breath. It was finally time to tell him the truth.

"Remember when I went with you to Amanda's cottage for the weekend?"

"How could I forget," he replied, secretly thinking that it was his most memorable conquests.

"You told me you loved me," she went on.

Jacy turned away and began to fidget. Right away she

knew what that meant. It had all been a ploy to get her into bed, and the reality of that thought caused her heart to ache. Before she went on, she wiped hot tears from her cheeks.

"You lied to me, didn't you?" Her voice trembled. For a long moment there was only silence and she added, "Well, I believed you… and I still love you."

Jacy stood up and turned away from her kicking a stone with his shoe.

"I didn't lie to you Jenny… I did love you… but that was a long time ago."

I did love you? She recited in her mind. *A long time ago? What the hell does that mean?* Anger welled up in her stronger than she even knew was possible, but she had to stay calm.

"I don't understand, Jacy?" She replied peering up at him. "You touched me and got excited just like the first time we met, and you kissed me like you did the day we made love."

Jacy pulled out a cigarette and lit it. After taking a couple of puffs, he bent down and offered it to her. With a sad look, she shook her head no.

"I don't know what to tell you," he said letting smoke drift out of his nose. "Yes, you still excite me."

Jenny stood up shaking. "I'm pregnant!" She blurted out, and her eyes searched his face.

He registered no emotion and just stared at her blankly. Then he threw down his butt and ground it into the gravel.

"What?" He asked, as if he hadn't heard.

"I'm pregnant Jacy, and yes- you are the father. I haven't been with anyone else."

Acting dizzy he slowly fell to the ground. He closed his eyes and for a good ten minutes laid in silence. He was usually so careful and wondered how this could have happened.

"So what are you going to do about it?" Jacy asked bluntly, stabbing her heart.

She wasn't about to let him off the hook that easily.

"You mean what are WE going to do about it," she corrected.

He laughed uneasily and it was clear to her that he did not see this situation as his problem.

"No, I mean what are YOU going to do," he repeated.

Her blood boiled rising into her cheeks.

§

Jenny recalled when she first told her father, and his immediate reaction was to kill Jacy. Jim did not trust him from the beginning, and never wanted his daughter to go out with him. But Jenny begged, and because of his love for his daughter, he conceded.

She told her father that the pregnancy was also her fault. She should have gone to the church retreat and not lied to be with Jacy. Then her father asked her the same thing: What are you going to do?

Jenny knew from a conversation with her doctor that she did have options. She could have an abortion, give the baby up for adoption, or keep it. The doctor asked her what she was going to do. To many people asking her the same question, *what are you going to do?*

§

Jenny had already spent a couple of hours after school with Jacy, and she knew her parents would worry if she were gone much longer. "Please drive me home," she said coldly.

Along the way she realized that she was entirely alone in her decision. As Jacy drove quietly, she felt frightened by the thought, and knew that because of the pregnancy her world would never be the same. His on the other hand, could go on as it always had.

He pulled in front of her house and she flashed a nervous smile. He kissed her cheek and said goodbye. She wanted to ask if she would see him again, but did not have the courage. As he drove away she already knew the answer.

18. Sharing The News

When a couple of months had passed, Jenny's baby bump became obvious. Of course Kristina figured out that she was pregnant, and at first she made her feel badly about it. Her mother then stepped in and reminded Kristina that many people had sex before marriage; the only difference was that some did not get caught. Marie did not know if Kristina was sexually active, but she acted much nicer after that.

Meanwhile Marie decided it was time to let the rest of Jenny's siblings know what was happening. Calling them into the living room she paced the floor trying to find the right words to tell Jessica, Erik and Regina. She could not help feeling uneasy. Erik still had homework to complete and wanted to get on with it. Then he could relax for the evening and listen to music.

"Come on, mom," he urged, "What do you want to tell us?"

"Okay, kids," she began, "I have some news for you, and I'm not sure how you're going to take it." For a moment she paused to gather her thoughts. She knew she had to deal with this delicately.

"Is it good news or bad news?" Jessica asked.

By this time Marie was beside herself trying to find the best way to say that their sister was going to have a baby. She had always taught them from the Bible: marriage before babies. And she had not even explained sex to them yet!

"Well, that depends…" Marie replied.

"What does that mean?" Erik interceded.

Marie drew a deep breath and glanced at her son who sat cross-legged on the couch with his arms tightly crossed.

"All right, it's like this," she began, but no more words escaped her mouth.

"Don't worry, mom," Regina said. "Whatever it is, we won't be mad at you." Marie moved beside her and ran her fingers through her hair.

"Thanks honey, but this is not about me. This is about your sister."

All eyes shot toward Jessica and she waved her hands in front of her face. "Don't look at me," Jessica said. "I have no idea what mom's talking about."

Erik grumbled under his breath growing ever more irritated.

"Now listen," Marie said, "This is about Jenny."

"Is she sneaking out again?" Erik asked. "I don't want to hear it." Sighing loudly he added, "I'm never having kids!"

"No she is not sneaking out."

Marie realized that the kids were restless and knew she'd better get to the point.

"Can you tell her belly is getting big?"

"Yeah, she shouldn't be eating so much," Erik responded, causing Marie to giggle under her breath. "…and we care why?"

"We all need to care, because your sister is pregnant."

Erik's eyes and mouth fell wide open, but he said nothing. As for Jessica, all she could muster was, "W-w-w-what?" Regina just stared at her mother curiously, and

Marie was not sure if she truly understood.

"You mean to tell me Jenny got knocked up?" Erik asked.

"Don't talk like that in front of your sisters," Marie insisted.

"So you're not mad that she's pregnant?" He asked, throwing his hands in the air in obvious frustration.

"What's done is done, Erik." She rubbed her temples feeling a migraine coming on and then added "Now we have no choice but to move on from here."

"Get outta here!" Regina exclaimed. "She can't be pregnant. She isn't even married yet." She searched her mother's eyes for more answers, but Marie was not sure she had any.

"Well, she is pregnant sweetie," Marie confirmed as she stroked her silky hair. Tears spilling down her cheeks she added, "To be entirely honest, you can get pregnant without being married. I never told you this before because it's just wrong. The way God intends it is for a couple to get married first, and then have children."

"Okay, so why are you crying mom?" Regina asked.

Marie wrapped her arms around her daughter, and gently rocked her back and forth "Because I did not know how to tell you that."

"I don't understand?" Regina replied as Erik and Jessica huddled around her.

"Mom is saying that you'll soon be like a big sister, except the baby will be Jenny's, not moms," Erik tried to explain.

"When is the baby coming?" Jessica asked in an unsure tone.

"In February, I think… but for now she needs your support. Don't be angry with her. She has a lot on her mind so try to be there for her. We have to make the best of this situation and I think – in time – we will all be able to do that."

After spilling the news to her children, Marie felt a huge sense of relief. For the first time she began to feel the joy of soon becoming a grandmother. She had been so worried about Jenny and the other children that she hadn't thought of that. However, Jenny still had a big decision to make. As far as Marie was concerned, abortion was not an option, but she still had to decide whether she would keep the baby. Marie was determined not to interfere, and made it clear that she would stand behind her no matter what she intended to do. She also decided to take Jenny shopping for maternity clothes and was surprised when she opted for oversized clothes rather than those labeled maternity.

"They're so ugly mom, and only older people wear them," she said.

§

By October it was clearly obvious to everyone that Jenny was pregnant. Marie thought it rather strange that some of the folks at church chose to ignore her and wondered why having a pregnant daughter was still such a huge taboo. One Sunday she walked into her church group where teen pregnancy was being discussed. All of the women in the group were between the ages of 30 and 50. Some were married, some divorced, and others lived alone.

While they were all different in their own way, they did have one thing in common; they were all close-minded. As she sat amid them, Marie gazed around and wondered *had any of them had sex before they were married? What about smoking or drinking? Did any of them ever do those types of things that were unacceptable to the church? And was there a difference between sins? Was one worse than the other? What if you asked for forgiveness? Did the heavenly Father forgive and wipe the slate clean?*

As her mind wandered back to the conversation one of the women raised the fact that the school provided a nursery for the children of teenage girls. Even if the school did not officially stand behind those girls, Marie thought the nursery was a wonderful idea. However, not everyone agreed.

"What's wrong with them?" Asked one woman. "The school system is just condoning sexual activity."

Marie listened in shock as a discussion ensued on how promiscuous teenage girls had become.

"They should not be allowed to return to school when they get pregnant," another woman noted before adding, "They should stay home with their babies. Motherhood brings new responsibilities, and their education should be put on the back burner."

Strangely, no one mentioned that it takes two to create a baby. *What about the boys who helped cause the pregnancy? Should they be discriminated against too? Why was all the pressure – and blame – placed squarely on the girl?* It was difficult for Marie to remain silent during this discourse, but she knew she must be discreet. However, it hurt her soul to hear them speak so harshly.

After church Marie stopped at the grocery store to purchase some items for dinner. The woman at the cash register asked if she was Jenny's mother. As she placed the items on the counter, Marie immediately felt nervous. She did not like the tone of the woman's voice.

"Yes," she answered.

"Is your daughter still living with you?" The woman

asked, causing Marie to look at her quizzically.

What a strange question, she thought, but the woman was not finished yet.

"I'm just asking because when my daughter got pregnant, I made her live on her own. She made her bed so she had to lie in it. That's how I felt." The woman finished putting the items into a bag and Marie paid her.

"What about the baby?" Marie asked before she walked away.

"I really don't know," she replied with a laugh. "That's her problem now, isn't it? It's called tough love and you need to do the same."

Marie left the store feeling judged by a total stranger because she took care of her 'promiscuous' daughter but she knew she could never abandon Jenny like that. In fact, she knew her daughter needed her family's support now more than ever.

What kind of a world would we live in if we simply judged others and did not try to help them? She wondered. Especially when those who need us are members of our own family! She was determined right then and there to be there for her children with her total love and compassion – no matter what.

19. Crash Course In Motherhood

Over the next couple of months Jenny watched her tummy swell larger and larger, along with her breasts. She could not help feeling uneasy as she had to wear bigger and bigger clothes. This was all so new to her. It was an experience she never considered or expected to have, especially while still a high school student. The stares she received from the other students did not help either. She detested how some of the teens gawked at her when she walked down the halls.

At the same time she was trying her hardest not to be angry with Jacy. It was not his choice or hers to have this happen. To be honest, she felt guilty about accepting his invitation to skip the church trip to be with him. She was the one who made that decision – one that seemed destined to change her life forever. The news that she was expecting came as quite a shock to him, and Jenny knew he needed time to adjust.

The guys at school gave Jacy a hard time as well.

"So you knocked Jenny up, eh stud?" They teased. "You're gonna be a daddy now. What are you going to do?"

Jacy could not simply ignore their words. When he saw how mean some people were to Jenny, he knew he had to step up to the plate and be a man about it. When he walked her to class, he heard the whispers around them. He saw the pain in her face as she tried to ignore them, and that hurt him too. He attempted to face his responsibility by treating her especially nice, driving her home each day after school and comforting her whenever she needed him. Somewhere along the way his feelings for her took an abrupt turn. He did not expect to care so much.

As she grew larger, Jenny received mixed emotions from her family. One day Kristina teased her for being so stupid and not making sure Jacy put on a rubber. The next day she acted benevolently and even asked her if she had picked out boys or girls names yet. Erik told her that he got teased at school for having a loose sister. Jessica did not seem to care one way or the other how Jenny handled the situation. In fact, she acted as if nothing had changed. Regina being the youngest seemed jealous as if she wanted all the attention. As for Marie and Jim, they tried to give Jenny the courage to go through this difficult time without any pressure. They did not even ask what she intended to do about the baby. They just wanted her to know that they were there for her.

Of course, Jenny had to tell the school administration that she was pregnant and ask how they could help her with her education. It was a real eye opener to learn that the school would stand behind her along with other girls going through the same thing. They added on a class to help prepare her for motherhood. She took a shuttle bus every day to a house nearby where other unwed teenagers tended to their babies.

The house had a big living area and a couple of bedrooms with a kitchen and bathroom. The living room was decorated with big brown teddy bears drawn on the walls. One of the bedrooms was painted in blue and the other in pink. Mrs. Smith, a thin woman in her 60's with her hair up in a bun and wearing blue jeans was in charge. When Jenny arrived, she greeted her cheerfully. There were seven babies from three months to a year in age either in playpens or cribs. She noticed four students changing diapers, feeding or rocking babies.

Mrs. Smith explained that she was pregnant in school and had been treated like an outcast.

"Back in those days if a student became pregnant she was shipped off to a relative in a different state. She would have the baby and give it up for adoption before being allowed to come back to school," she said shaking her head in disgust. "She was not allowed to finish high school if she decided to keep her child."

Mrs. Smith said she had her baby and went on to get her high school credits later in life. At the time, she promised herself that this would not happen to any young girl in trouble again. She wanted to create a course to help young mothers acquire some experience taking care of a baby before they gave birth. She also hoped to help those girls get their high school diplomas.

To Jenny's surprise there were more teenage mothers than she thought, and seeing the small and delicate babies was an emotional experience. One girl named Tammy sat bottle-feeding her baby. When she said hello to Jenny, she noticed that her long brown hair was pulled back into a ponytail. She looked far too young to be a mother, but she delicately held her baby and rocked him.

"Hi, I'm Jenny," she replied. "It's a boy, right?"

"One thing to remember," she said with a laugh, "...the boys are usually in blue and girls are usually wearing pink."

The baby finished his bottle so Tammy gently put him over her shoulder. She made sure to hold her baby's head so it would not bounce, and gently patted his back.

"What are you doing?" Jenny asked.

"I'm burping him. He can't digest his food by himself yet so I have to help him."

When the baby burped, Jenny just stared.

"Want to hold him?" Tammy asked.

"You don't mind?"

"No," she said standing to hand the baby over to her. Jenny clumsily put her arms out not sure how to hold him.

"Put one hand under his head and the other under his body," she explained. She carefully placed the baby in Jenny's arms and her body tensed up. She was afraid she might break the little infant but Tammy just smiled.

"Don't worry," she said kindly. "He's a lot stronger than he looks!"

As she began to relax she closed her eyes taking in a whiff of the baby. The smell was so delightful, and holding the baby changed her entire attitude about being pregnant. She could not wait to share this experience with Jacy.

"What's his name?" Jenny whispered as the baby tried to sleep.

"Tony," she said. "After his father."

Jenny quickly looked up. "Is he helping with the baby?"

"Oh, yeah," she replied smiling. "At first he wasn't sure he wanted anything to do with a baby. In fact, he tried to talk me into getting an abortion, but I told him I could not just kill him. I was on my own at first until I had him, but once Tony saw the baby, he fell in love. Now we're waiting for me to graduate so we can get married."

Tammy took the baby from Jenny's arms and put him in a crib in the blue room.

"I don't believe in abortions either," Jenny said. "But I

haven't decided if I want to keep my baby or give it up for adoption."

"What about the father?" Tammy asked with sad eyes. "Is he involved?"

Jenny cringed before she answered. "I don't think so. He told me this was my problem." Tammy leaned over and gave her a warm hug.

"Give him some time," she suggested. "Tony finally came around. Bring him here to see these little ones. I bet he'll change his mind."

Tammy then introduced Jenny to three other girls. She met Michelle, a senior with a 9-month-old baby girl that already had a full head of curly brown hair. She said her boyfriend's involvement was sporadic at best. Sometimes he wanted to be a part of his daughter's life, and other times he didn't. She explained that at first she moved in with him and it was fun pretending they were married. However, he soon became angry because the baby cried all the time and she had to give her all of her attention. Then he started partying again, not coming home or arriving home drunk. Then she knew that she should go back home. The baby needed a stable place to live, one without irritation and one where she would be loved. Fortunately, her parents gladly took her back.

Next she met Lynn, a senior with an 11-month-old baby boy. Lynn said her parents were very distressed over her pregnancy and kicked her out when they found out. She said she did not know the father. Her grandparents agreed to take her in, which she really appreciated except that she was not allowed to go out. They were in their '70s, so she had to be with her baby all the time. Due to their health, they were in no position to take care of her or her child. Lynn said she missed being able to go to parties, but realized that was the price of being a mother.

Last she met Roz, a junior with her 3-month-old baby girl who had a little bit of white, straight hair around her head. Roz said she was married to the baby's father and lived with his parents who were very kind. However, they never had any privacy. His mom always ran to the baby's room whenever she heard her cry and constantly told her what she was doing wrong. Roz said she felt inadequate trying to finish school and be a good mother at the same time.

Jenny left the house with an empty feeling inside and wondered what her future held. She knew that would depend on what choice she made. *Should she keep her baby and be a mother? If so, how was she going to care for the child? And was Jacy going to be part of her future too?* So many questions that, for the time being, had no answers.

§

Reality hit home with Marie and Jim when Jenny told them that Jacy wanted to be a part of her life while she was pregnant. She still had not decided if she would keep the baby, but until then, she wanted Jacy to experience everything with her. Her parents only wanted the best for her, so they decided to allow him to engage in the family's activities.

Jacy could not believe how much beauty Jenny radiated as her tummy began to grow. He continued to drive her home from school, and often stayed for dinner. On Friday nights he joined the family to watch movies. On one of those nights, the unexpected happened.

They were all relaxing and watching Star Wars together when Jenny reacted strangely. She was about to take a bite of pizza, but before she even put it to her mouth, she made an odd sound. She immediately sat up and placed a hand on her tummy.

"What is it dear?" Marie asked, always keeping an eagle eye on her daughter.

"I'm not sure?" Jenny sat back again and picked up her pizza. She took a bite and was chewing on it when she felt something strange again. She swiftly sat up straight with her back off the couch.

"Are you all right?" Jacy asked looking worried. He placed a hand softly on the middle of her back.

"Yes," she giggled, "but I think the baby just moved!"

Marie jumped from her seat and ran over to her daughter. Jacy quickly shuffled over so she could sit between them. Since everyone's attention turned to Jenny, Jim put the movie on pause.

"Where?" Marie asked excitedly, her hands exploring her tummy. She was quite literally bouncing with joy. The biggest thing she missed about being pregnant five times herself was feeling the baby kicking inside of her.

"Here," Jenny replied placing her mother's hands over the spot.

They all sat quietly waiting for any sign of movement again. It seemed like forever and Erik started to get antsy.

"Oh!" Cried Marie, smiling from ear to ear. "I felt it!"

Rising from the couch she motioned for Jacy to move back over. He was not sure what was happening, but he let Marie put his hand over the same area. Jenny placed her hand over his and glanced up at him contentedly.

"Let me feel," squealed Jessica rushing over to kneel in front of her sister.

"In a minute," she said. Then it happened. Jacy felt something and glanced quickly at Jenny looking scared.

"What was that?"

"Our baby, silly!" Jenny giggled. He started rubbing around her tummy looking for more movement.

"My turn," Jessica insisted and tried to push Jacy out of the way.

"Let her have a turn," Jenny urged and Jacy reluctantly let go. Jessica placed her hands on her tummy and waited.

"Okay," Erik interrupted impatiently. "We all know the baby is moving. Now can we switch back to the movie?"

He already had two little sisters, so Jenny's pregnancy was really not important to him. Jim put the movie back on and everyone settled in again. Jacy moved closer to Jenny and put his arm around her. With his other hand he quietly moved back to the spot on her belly secretly hoping to feel movement again. Jenny rested her head on his shoulder and quietly cried inside. Her baby moved - such a beautiful moment to share with Jacy, *but how long would it last?* She wondered?

20. A Difficult Decision

Time seemed to speed up as Jenny's life filled with doctor's appointments and birthing classes, which Jacy attended with her. She loved spending an hour each day at the school nursery taking care of the babies. Even though she had become too big to have little ones sit on her lap, she still loved her time with them. She also enjoyed long talks with the other teenage mothers on why they decided to keep their babies. It sounded like such a hard job with no personal time to spare.

They told her about nights with no sleep when the baby cried constantly, not to mention the midnight feedings. During the day they had doctor's appointments to keep, and countless diapers to change. They related their frustrations, but ensured that she also knew the positive side of motherhood and the rewards of raising a child. They unanimously agreed that they made the right decision to keep their babies.

Mrs. Smith gave Jenny the names of some of the teens that gave their babies up for adoption. She suggested that after talking to them, she might be more able to make a choice. The number of girls who actually did this surprised her. Walking the school hallways one would never know which of the girls were ever pregnant. Some were reluctant to talk, and upset that she even asked them to explain themselves. Others however, were more than happy to share their stories. The reasons they offered for giving up their babies were wide-ranging. Some said that although they did not believe in abortion, they were not ready to become parents. It was hard enough to grow up by yourself, let alone as a teen mother. Some said they had definite plans for the future, and a baby could not be a part of their lives at that point. Of course, they did not think about becoming pregnant when they slept with their boyfriends, so it came as a total surprise; one that they were not prepared to accept. Some of the girls simply did not want a baby. They slept around and thought they were careful. They knew the consequences, but thought they were protected.

"Isn't it funny when you take the pill religiously, but you still get pregnant?" Asked one of the girls. "I knew that this child was supposed to be here, but I was not ready to be a mother. There are a lot of women looking for babies, and I blessed one of them with mine."

Some girls said they had no family support or the baby's father would not help them, so in the best interest of the child, they gave it up.

"My mother threw me out of the house when she found out I was pregnant," said another girl. "After the baby was born I put her up for adoption. My mother called me a couple of weeks later and asked what happened to my baby. I let her know that she had different parents, and my mother told me I could come back home."

One couple told Jenny that their parents made them give up the baby. However, as soon as they finished high school, they planned to marry and try to have a family of their own. They also wanted to find the baby they lost.

The messages from these girls were all so different, but they agreed that it was better to have the baby and give the child up to a loving set of parents than to opt for abortion. After talking extensively to them, Jenny wanted to know why anyone would choose abortion and kill a baby. To find the answer, she decided to visit an abortion clinic.

The next day, she entered a clinic and spotted a petite woman sitting behind the desk. The lady in charge was happy to answer her questions. She noted that she had an abortion herself when she was 18. She said many girls had abortions because they did not feel ready for motherhood. Some did not have family support to help raise their child and others just could not afford it on their own. She added that she still remembered the relief mixed with sadness that she experienced, and that most girls who make this decision suffer from guilt, shame, and regret.

Jenny could easily see the pain on her face when she said the birthday of her unborn child would be etched in her memory forever. She thanked the woman for her time and could not get out of the clinic fast enough. She needed to talk to Mrs. Smith. When she shared what she had learned, Mrs. Smith cried.

"Those poor children," she sobbed.

§

One day after school Amanda approached Jenny at her locker.

"So you got knocked up, eh?" She asked throwing back a long, blonde braid. "What ya going to do about it?"

"What do you mean?" Jenny asked curiously.

"Are you going to have an abortion?"

"What kind of a question is that?"

Amanda's face went blank and she motioned for Jenny to follow her. They walked outside to a grassy spot with a tree a little ways away. Amanda sat down and then patted the ground for her to sit as well.

"Why are we out here?"

Amanda looked sad and folded her hands neatly on her lap.

"I have a confession to make," she said. She tilted her head as if trying to find the right words.

"I had an abortion, and I would advise you not to do it," she confided as a gentle wind blew her hair across her face – hiding her tears.

Jenny was stunned and gasped aloud. Then she quickly covered her mouth wishing she hadn't. She did not intend to make Amanda feel any worse than she already did.

"I can tell what you are thinking Jenny, but you don't really know anything about me," she said wiping away tears that spilled from her eyes. "Please don't judge me," she added pushing some hair behind her ear. "I did not have a choice."

Jenny waited patiently for Amanda to continue.

"Remember when I told you I had sex once before?"

Jenny nodded, but was not sure she wanted to know more about that. As a sign of comfort, she cupped Amanda's hands in hers.

"You don't have to tell me anything," she offered. Her eyes scanned Amanda's face. She looked tired and her mascara was starting to run with the tears that fell. She did not want to see Amanda in pain. Nor did she want to raise painful memories from Amanda's past.

"Yes I do," Amanda gasped. "I thought I was in love." Although she wanted to look straight at Jenny, she could barely see through a veil of tears.

"So one night under pressure I made love with him. The man I thought was my knight in shining armor - the only man I thought knew and loved me. When I didn't get my period I told him I might be pregnant. He told me the baby could not be his. I didn't understand why he said that." She breathed out heavily and wiped her hands on her pants.

"He called me a whore and told me he didn't want me in his life," she said, her body shaking. "So I told my mom and she made an appointment for me to see a doctor." Amanda began to tremble uncontrollably.

"She said I should have an abortion and forget him, rather than have another mouth to feed. I still remember that day and the procedure still haunts me."

Jenny rose to her knees and hugged her friend. "It's okay," she said.

"Jenny, I am so ashamed. Because of this, I have so much guilt and regret on my heart. I just wanted to share what happened with you so you don't make the same mistake."

For a while they held each other in silence. When they finally parted, Jenny thanked Amanda for her honesty and promised not to share her story with anyone.

That afternoon Jenny and Jacy walked hand-in-hand in the mall. They stopped at a store window to look at baby furniture and then wondered if they should go inside another shop to check out baby clothes. She enjoyed playing a game of a mom and a dad looking for stuff for their baby, but at the same time the pretence hurt her inside.

Afterward they stopped at the food court to grab a bite to eat. Each time a stroller rolled by, Jenny could not help peaking inside. With piped-in music, people chatting, and children crying, it was quite noisy and not conducive to conversation. However, Jenny had plenty on her mind. Time was short and she needed to talk.

"We need to discuss whether I should give up the baby," she said, hoping no one else heard. Taking a sip of her drink she added, "Do you want me to keep the baby?"

Jacy played with his food while he considered the question. He knew this conversation was coming and he'd gone over the options many times. While he would love to have said, "It's your baby. Do what you want," that answer just did not seem right anymore. Even though the baby was not born yet, he had grown attached in a way he'd never expected.

Jacy recalled a recent visit to her doctor. He held her hand while the technician conducted an ultra sound. She placed a wand on Jenny's tummy, and when he looked at the monitor he could not believe his eyes. The image was so clear that he could count the baby's fingers and toes. He also heard the baby's heartbeat, and it was the greatest experience of his life. There really was a living being inside of her, and it was a baby that they had created together.

Jacy had also learned that Jenny was a good person, and always brought out the best in him. He was no longer the carefree don't-give-a-damn teenager that he was just one year before.

"What do you want to do?" He said finally.

"I'm still not sure," she said honestly. "Are we too young to take on the responsibility of caring for a baby?"

In her heart Jenny hoped he would tell her everything was all right. She needed to hear that he wanted to be a part of their baby's life, and that he would be there to help her.

"Maybe… maybe not," he replied as a smile grew on his face.

With that response, Jenny felt for the first time that there was hope for them. As he took her hand in his tears welled up in her eyes.

"I love you Jenny," he said.

Jenny swore he looked right into her soul.

"I love you too, Jacy."

They leaned in for a hug with no thought of other people around them. At that moment they shared their joy and the world seemed a happy place.

"So what do we do now?" She asked wiping the tears from her face.

"We have to take care of our baby!" He whispered.

That night Jacy tossed and turned as he considered his future. He pictured himself as the father of a little boy, showing him how to do such things as holding and tossing a ball and the thought of it made him feel good inside. He never planned to become involved with anyone. He just wanted to have fun, have sex, and go on his way. But now he could barely remember the selfish, self-centered person that he used to be. He had grown and matured in so many ways.

As Jenny's belly grew and he felt the life inside of her, he knew a miracle was about to occur. They were having a baby! Of course, they still had sex occasionally, but it was no longer just for the thrill of it. He truly felt a connection to Jenny and realized that there was so much more to life.

The guys at school continued to taunt him about becoming a father but it did not annoy him anymore. He just smiled to himself; yes he was going to be a father with the most beautiful woman he knew, and she was the mother of his child. He knew no one understood him like she did, and he fully acknowledged how much he needed her to be a major part of his life.

Jacy had not seen the old gang since the summer before. He spent his vacation on the reservation and when he returned to the city, he no longer needed to depend on

Amanda to get around because he had his own truck. Amanda still hung around with Susan, Sandy and Gary, but Jacy felt he had outgrow them. He still waved to them in the school halls and stopped to chat sometimes, but his priorities had changed.

Jacy spent much of his time with Jenny and her family but on one occasion he broke a rule in that household: abstinence from smoking pot. When this came to light he discerned that her parents had done plenty of soul searching before they would allow him back into their home. At first he felt uncomfortable, but Jenny's touch assured him of their acceptance. Over time he knew he'd again become like one of the family.

Friday nights with her family having pizza and watching television became an activity that he looked forward to and enjoyed. It amused him to watch Jenny's siblings play and fight, but more importantly, he saw how her parents treated each other so tenderly and he wanted that too.

Jenny's family life was light years away from what he'd known as a child. His mother worked full time so he learned to take care of himself. He could not remember ever seeing his parents look at each other like Marie and Jim. Back then he lived in two different worlds – one with his mom and another with his dad. On the reservation his father made huts for a living and his life was a poor one. He enjoyed hunting with his dad and learning to be a good woodsman. His mother on the other hand, worked hard to keep a roof over his head and food on his plate. There was little time to spend with her and although he understood why, he knew something was missing. With Jenny's family he found that missing piece.

One Friday evening after the movie ended and

everyone else left the living room, Jenny turned to Jacy. Her mother told her they could stay and talk for another thirty minutes so she snuggled up next to him.

"Did you want a baby?" She asked out of the blue.

"I'm not sure I understand what you're asking."

"I mean, did you ever think of having children?" She asked looking deeply into his eyes.

"Are you asking if I want this baby?" He asked obviously confused.

She nodded in the affirmative.

"This is our baby. We made him. Of course I want him."

"That's not what I mean."

"Well to be honest, I never really thought about children," he replied finally getting her drift. "I suppose I wanted marriage and children someday."

Jenny moved closer and put her head on Jacy's shoulder.

"Are you happy?" She whispered.

Jacy thought for a moment. Happiness had taken on a whole new meaning over the past year.

"Yes, I am," he whispered back.

The following week, Jenny coaxed Jacy into visiting the school nursery with her. He felt as if he were in a different world with the teddy bear walls and soft Disney music playing in the background. She eagerly introduced him to Mrs. Smith and the girls who were taking care of babies. He could not help noticing the other girls and watched intently as they held, fed or sung to the little ones. When a baby cried, he saw how tender and compassionate they were toward the infants. They made tending to them look so easy. He could feel the love in that house and just being there made him feel more comfortable with his own situation. But the biggest surprise to him was the number of teenage mothers. He was not alone, and decided that he would be more than happy in this world.

21. The Big News

One afternoon Jenny and Jacy asked her parents to join them in the living room so they could talk. As everyone sat down, Marie looked uneasy. Jim noticed her nervousness and took her hand in his. Jenny circled the room wringing her hands. She had never felt so nervous – except perhaps the night she told her mother she was pregnant. She was not sure how her parents would take her news. They had been most accepting and supportive to that point and she did not want to push them over the limit. However, what she was about to ask for was something she yearned for more than life itself. She appreciated that they never pressure her about her decision and had treated her like an adult. Jacy sat quietly leaving Jenny in charge of the conversation.

"Mom, dad," she began clasping her hands together in a tight ball.

Marie involuntarily held her breath as if afraid of what might come next.

"I made my decision," she continued, and moved closer to Jacy. She took his hand and looked into his dark brown eyes.

"We have decided that we want to keep this gift from God."

She noticed Jacy squirm in his seat and squeezed his hand reassuringly. Then she turned toward her parents who beamed with joy. It was obvious that they were pleased with her news. Marie jumped up to give Jenny a hug.

"My grandbaby," she squealed putting her hands on her daughter's stomach. "Do you hear me little one. I'm your grandmother!"

Jenny felt like a thousand weights were lifted from her shoulders. Jacy sat back in his seat and sighed with relief. Marie gave her daughter a kiss on the cheek and then offered Jacy a big hug.

"Thank you," she said. "Thank you for allowing this baby to be a part of our lives."

Marie had always said that giving birth was one of the happiest moments in her life besides getting married. She said God had graced her with five children, something that would always cause her to be grateful. However, she had no idea how thrilling it might be to learn she would be a grandmother. She no longer thought about Jenny being so young and unmarried. It was the baby-to-be that now consumed her world.

Marie told Jenny about her first pregnancy at 21. She had been on the pill but Jim found the container with a lot of pills left at the end of the month. She did not purposely forget to take them. Knowing little about how they worked if she skipped a day or two, she just took more when she realized what she had done. Of course, this did not work! After missing her period for a couple of months she went to the doctor. A pregnancy test revealed that she was due in six months! Jim could hardly believe it. They had only been married a couple of years and a baby would certainly throw a wrench into their plans. They wanted to do some traveling across the United States before they had children, but were then forced to change their plans and prepare for parenthood.

Marie recalled how discouraged she was at first when

she gained weight because her clothes did not fit properly. But as time went on she enjoyed shopping for maternity clothes. Like any mom-to-be she was thrilled when she first felt life inside of her. When it began, she wondered if the slight flutters she felt might only be food digesting. It was such a strange feeling. But soon those flutters were kicks and she knew her baby was getting stronger.

Marie's first pregnancy was not an easy one because she had a rare blood disease. At any time it could cause her blood count to drop dangerously low. To counteract this, the doctor put her on iron shots. Unfortunately, they did not work and she had to have a blood infusion. She related that her labor lasted eighteen hours and said she hoped her daughter would not have to go through that.

"In the end though, the pain was well worth the reward," she said, "...a beautiful baby girl that was seven pounds, four ounces."

When Marie examined her baby for the first time she was thrilled to find ten fingers and ten toes. As she touched her baby's soft skin and listened to her cry, she said it was a sensation she would never forget.

At Jenny's next doctor's appointment a small problem was discovered. Another ultra sound revealed that the placenta was covering part of the cervical opening – something called placenta previa. The doctor explained that this could start without warning - no pain - just bleeding but she also assured them that everything would probably be fine.

"Since this didn't start until the end of her second trimester, it should correct itself," the doctor noted.

However, the doctor warned Jenny that if she began to bleed severely she would have to deliver the baby right away - even if it was premature. Most likely she would need a c-section and be given blood. Jenny saw the fearful look on Marie's face over what might happen to her daughter and her grandchild. She had not told her daughter about the baby she'd lost at only two months pregnant. It would have been her third child…

One day Marie was working in the beauty shop when she felt some pressure and a little pain in her abdomen. She went to the bathroom, sat down and caught the embryo in her hand.

"I can still see the tiny fish-like form of a face enclosed in a clear bubble and caught on a big blood clot," she said. "It was devastating."

Needless to say, she could not imagine her daughter losing her baby. She also knew that since Jenny was so young she was considered a high-risk pregnancy case. The doctor put her on bed rest so she had to be home schooled. Twice a week a teacher came by to see her. She was most thankful that the school was so caring about its students. The teachers wanted everyone, including expectant teens, to succeed and went out of their way to help them.

Although Marie looked forward to the birth of her grandchild, one question haunted her. *What would it be like when the baby finally arrived?* Jenny and Jacy were not married, and listened to Marie when she suggested that they wait until they graduated. She wanted them to be sure they were truly in love but she still had some lingering concerns about Jacy because of his past behavior. He was the one who coaxed Jenny to smoke, drink, and lie to her parents. He would never have been the person Marie chose for her daughter. She knew the Bible said to forgive others and show God's love, but that was easier said than done.

However, Marie realized how much Jenny loved him, and saw how loving Jacy acted toward her. Her daughter was having his baby, so she decided that it was more important to forgive, be there for them, and offer them a happy and peaceful environment for them and for their baby-to-be.

22. The Holidays

As the holidays drew near, the weather turned cold and snowy. Jenny was more than happy to stay inside in her enlarged condition. Her increased weight caused her ankles to swell and her back to ache. She often watched television with her legs propped up to reduce both the swelling and pain. Sleeping became difficult because she could not get comfortable lying on her back, or on her side. Not to mention the frequent visits to the bathroom.

Being inside so much, she frequently grew bored and looked forward to the times her teachers arrived to bring her homework. Some of the girls from the school's nursery also dropped in to visit. They brought along their babies, which Jenny enjoyed. Holding and cuddling the infants made her anxious to have her own little one.

Jenny still looked forward to Friday nights when the family joined together, but the best days were those when Jacy dropped by. He brought her cards and notes from the kids at school, and always asked what he could do to help her feel more comfortable. Sometimes he sat and rubbed her back or feet to make them feel better. Their love was growing and it showed in so many ways.

Jenny also looked forward to the holidays when her siblings would be home more often, and Jacy would be off school so he could spend more time with her. The excitement of Christmas was in the air. With help from

Kristina and Erik, Jim and Marie placed lights all around the house. Jim climbed onto the roof to put up white icicle lights, while Marie placed big old-fashioned colored lights around the edge of the roof. Erik made sure the bushes and trees around the house were decorated in lights as well. Kristina set up a display in the front yard with small blue lights that looked like a stream, and placed a deer enjoying a drink.

Meanwhile Jenny and Jessica baked chocolate chip and sugar cookies, and Regina decorated them. The oven made the house extra warm and the baking cookies sent a wonderful scent wafting throughout the house. Jenny decided to make hot chocolate to go along with the cookies for everyone working in the cold outside.

The holidays would not be complete without Christmas shopping. The malls were packed and bursting with holiday spirit. As usual there was a Santa for the children and the mall was filled with the sound of Christmas music. To do their part to spread the joy of the season, Jenny and Jacy joined the church group to sing carols at a couple of nursing homes. The pastor showed no prejudice over their current state of affairs and welcomed them to take part. Jenny talked Jacy out of spending the holiday on the reservation.

Two days before Christmas Jim brought home a tree that they let stand all day. Jenny loved the smell of fresh pine. Early on the afternoon of Christmas Eve they decorated the tree while soft carols played in the background. Jacy and Jenny added multicolored Italian lights. It was a family tradition for other members of the family to join in as well.

Jessica tried to string popcorn but had trouble with it crumbling in her hands. Regina and Marie each grabbed a needle and thread to help her. Between the three of them they made three long strands of popcorn to put around the tree. It was pretty funny because there seemed to be more of the little morsels on the floor than on the tree!

Erik and Kristina took the ornaments out of their boxes. They made sure none were broken, and that each had a hook attached. If Erik had his way, the family would watch a horror flick while decorating the tree, so he just sat back and rolled his eyes as the others did their part.

"Is your mom coming with us to church tonight?" Jenny asked.

"Yep," Jacy said smiling. "She's very excited about it." They finally reached the end of the string of lights and plugged them in.

"Oh, they look so pretty," Jenny noted.

Jacy truly enjoyed this activity with the family. He realized that he was making new memories with Jenny - the woman he loved.

"Why is your mom so excited?" She asked.

"We usually spend Christmas by ourselves and we only have a table top tree, nothing like this one." He gazed at the tree with approval. He'd never seen one like it other than at the mall. "And we don't bake cookies," he added with a laugh. "Mom buys sugar ones from Wal-Mart." He stuck out his tongue and crinkled his nose.

Jacy loved it when Regina decorated the cookies and the fresh-baked smell overcame his senses. She asked him to help and it was the first time he ever put frosting and M & M's on cookies before he popped one in his mouth.

Marie's face displayed her joy at seeing her children, as well as Jacy, laughing and smiling while trimming the tree. She saw how tenderly he treated Jenny and how he helped her sit down on the couch. Jenny knew it likely brought back memories for her mother of when she was young and in love. She moved closer to Jacy to give him a hug but as usual her tummy got in the way. She grabbed him anyway, her stomach touched his and the baby moved.

"Hey, I felt that," he said and kissed her lightly on the cheek. "Hey you! Can you hear daddy's voice?"

Jacy knelt down, put his ear to her stomach, and placed his hands on both sides of her waist. Jenny laughed with amusement.

"I want to feel the baby," Regina insisted and jumped off the couch. The baby moved again causing her to scream with delight.

"My turn," said Jessica scrambling to her side.

"I'm your Aunt Jessica," she yelled at her tummy.

Marie laughed, obviously enjoying the actions of her children. It was not so long ago that things were quite different, but Jacy had become part of the family. After they all had a turn feeling the baby move, they put the finishing touches on the tree. Then they turned the lights on to see the product of their handiwork. For several moments no one said a word. They simply admired how beautiful it looked.

"Got to go now," Jacy said rising from the couch, "...but I'll be back with my mom in time for church."

With a quick kiss goodbye, he left the family to continue their festivities, but it turned out to be a quiet couple of hours. Jenny had grown tired and decided to catch a quick nap before getting ready for church. Marie kept busy in the kitchen preparing the food for that evening, while Jessica, Kristina and Regina watched the Christmas movie, Scrooge. Erik went to his room to watch Star Wars. Jim got off work early and after supper everyone got dressed. When Marie heard a knock at the door she answered it.

"Hi Marie," said Jacy. "This is my mom, Nancy."

As she walked in, Marie could see that she was a short woman and a little over weigh. Her smile was enchanting and she had Jacy's eyes.

"Glad to finally meet you," she said warmly.

"Thank you," Nancy replied handing over a box of Wal-Mart sugar cookies.

Jenny quickly descended the stairs to greet them, and noticed how handsome Jacy looked in his black shirt and pants. His black hair was combed neatly falling down around his shoulders. Jacy reached out to hold her hand and looked lovingly into her eyes. He noticed how beautiful she looked in her green jumper that stretched over her big belly and a white blouse with lace on the collar. She took his hand and followed him over to meet his mother.

"Mom," he sang with confidence in his voice, "this is my Jenny."

Nancy's glance drifted from her tummy back up to her face.

"I finally get to meet you," she said offering a warm embrace. "I've heard so much about you, Jenny. My son talks so highly of you."

"It's nice to meet you too, Mrs. Kavi."

Jenny introduced Nancy to all of her siblings before they left for church. The parking lot was full when they arrived and church members strolled into the building. Since it was so cold outside the warmth of the church made it even more inviting. Soft organ music played, the lights were dimmed, and fake candles on the walls lit up the sanctuary. A large Christmas tree with little white lights, big red bows, and silver ornaments sat up front. People hugged each other hello before the pastor took the podium.

The choir wore red robes and sang *God Rest You Merry Gentlemen*. After a few more songs, the pastor began his sermon.

He talked about the birth of our Lord and Savior, adding how important it was to show God's love to anyone and everyone we met. The choir director led the congregation through more Christmas carols and then the pastor said a prayer, lit a real candle, and gave it to the person in the first row who lit her candle. She passed the candle on and this continued until everyone lit his or her candle and the church glowed inside.

Marie and Jim held each other's hands and admired their five children. Jacy and his mother sat at the end of the row. He held hands with Jenny who looked radiant in the soft candlelight. Finally, they sang *What Child is This* before reciting the Lord's Prayer. The service ended with the pastor wishing everyone a happy holiday.

As they left the church little flakes of snow began to fall. Regina and Jessica tried to catch them on their tongues while Jacy gripped Jenny's arm to keep her from falling. When they arrived home everyone gathered in the kitchen. Marie put out her meal and the homemade cookies but before they ate, they said a short prayer of thankfulness.

Since the Christmas routine included watching *'It's A Wonderful Life,'* they nestled on the couch, sat on chairs or even plopped on the floor. It was also a family tradition to open one gift that night, so after the movie Marie passed them out. She even passed one to Nancy to make her feel at home. Jenny surprised Jacy and passed one to him too. His face lit up when she placed a green package with a red bow in his hand. It was a lighter with his name engraved on it. Jacy then reciprocated. He had wrapped his gift in white paper with a red bow on top, and it was the first one she ever received from a boy. When she unwrapped it, she saw a box from a jewelry store and looked up at him surprised.

"Open it," he coaxed.

Jenny's hands trembled as she lifted the top off the box and found a silver heart locket inside.

"Oh, my goodness!" She said.

Jacy gently took the locket from her, opened the latch and showed her a picture of him that was hidden inside.

"I don't have a picture of you, so could you put that in there too?" He asked.

"Of course!"

Tears filled her eyes as he placed the necklace around her neck.

"Thank you," she said softly and leaned over to kiss him.

It was around midnight when Jacy and his mother left. The family then settled in to get some sleep before the big day.

Early Christmas morning the children rushed from their beds to the tree in the living room. Presents were passed out, and the noise of paper being torn filled the room. Marie sat smiling and gazing at her children who where ripping open their presents with such glee. She knew this would be the last Christmas before the big arrival. Next year they would have another member of their family.

After everyone opened their presents Jim made breakfast. Then the adults opted for a short nap while the children watched movies. Jacy spent the day with his mother, but after dinner he joined Jenny's family on a trip to the movie theatre.

The day after Christmas there were many chores to do. All the crumbled wrapping paper had to be picked up, the floor vacuumed, the dishes washed, and the kitchen cleaned. Afterward everyone was exhausted, especially Jenny. She made her way slowly down the hall to her room holding a hand on her tummy as if she held up something heavy. She sat on her bed and let out a deep breath. It feels so good just to take off my shoes, she mused. She lied down flat but was so uncomfortable and moved to her right side to take the pressure off her back.

"Now be good baby," she mumbled closing her eyes to dream.

You know how it is when you close your eyes and don't even know you fell asleep? Then you open your eyes and complain to yourself that you haven't slept- before you notice the time and a couple of hours have passed? That's how Jenny felt. She got out of bed slowly and yawned. She needed to go to the bathroom and needed a glass of water. As she walked to the other end of the hall, she heard whispering.

"Kristina," Jenny muttered. "Is that you?"

She slid her feet along the carpet and held onto the railing as she made her way down the stairs. Then she heard giggling.

"Surprise!" Screamed a room full of girls and babies. Jenny's eyes opened wide as she spotted her mother, and Michelle, Lynn, Roz and Tammy with their little ones. Nancy was also there along with her mother and sisters. Then she saw the pink and blue streamers twisted on the ceiling, with balloons of the same colors in the corners of the room. A large bunch of them hung down in the middle.

"Come and sit down," Marie said ushering her daughter into the room. "We thought you were never going to wake up." She kissed her daughter on the forehead before placing her hands around her daughter's tummy and saying hello to her unborn grandchild.

"How long did I sleep?" Jenny asked wiping her eyes.

"Almost three hours," her mother answered. "We finally had to go into your room and make a little noise to wake you up."

"Wow, I didn't even think I fell asleep," she giggled.

After everyone greeted her, Jenny took a seat.

"Okay girls, it's time for games," shouted Kristina passing around bingo cards and pennies.

"You can use the pennies as spotters," she explained, "…but you should know that this is not an ordinary bingo game. This one has to do with babies."

Laughter and gossip filled the air as the games ensued. Afterward Marie brought out sandwiches and cake. Then Jenny opened her presents and there were plenty of oohs and aahs as she revealed tiny little shirts and sleepers. The biggest surprise was a car seat and even a baby crib. For Jenny, the afternoon seemed to fly by. She was so happy to spend this time with family and friends in celebration of the impending birth. Eventually the babies became restless and needed to go home.

When everyone left, the house seemed so quiet. Jenny and her mom, along with her siblings relaxed in the living room. Jim and Erik had gone to a movie during the baby shower and had not returned yet. Jenny picked up a receiving blanket and felt the softness of it against her cheek. She looked at some of her other gifts again, including the tiny undershirts.

"Were we ever that small?" Kristina asked, and Marie laughed aloud.

"Were our feet really this small?" Regina asked putting her finger inside one of the baby socks. "This could fit on one of my old baby dolls."

"Well, I like these little blanket sleepers," said Jessica

as she examined the opening for the feet. "This looks like a bag."

"It's kind of like a bag," Marie noted. "I miss having a baby around the house." Smiling at her daughter she added, "I love blanket sleepers. With these the baby can keep his legs wrapped together just like in the womb."

Jenny nodded, but did not really understand what her mother was talking about. Just then the front door opened, and Jim and Erik entered.

"So we missed the party?" Laughed Erik.

"You haven't missed everything," hinted Marie. She quickly glanced at a large box sitting by the wall. "You still have a job to do with your father."

Erik realized it was a crib that needed to be put together, and let out a groan. Luckily for him, Jim said it could wait until the following day.

23. Fearing The Worst

Jenny never expected to become pregnant when her family moved to Oklahoma. Nor did she imagine falling in love. But over time Jacy became not only her lover, but also her best friend. She did not want to live a day without talking to him or holding his hand. She had never experienced love before so she could not be sure, but if wanting to share her world with just one person meant anything, then she truly was in love. Whenever she thought of him, she smiled and whenever she thought about her baby-to-be, she grew ecstatic with anticipation.

I wonder if I'll have a boy or a girl? She thought rubbing her tummy.

They had decided to wait for the baby's arrival to find out. As her due date neared she also grew more and more nervous. She had attended birthing classes and during one of them a film was shown of a woman screaming when the baby's head appeared. The thought of all that pain frightened her, and even made her nauseous.

One day she asked her mother, "How much will it hurt to deliver the baby?"

Marie confided that Erik was her biggest baby at 8 pounds, 9 ounces. She told Jenny that after arriving too early to the hospital to have Kristina, she decided to wait at home until her labor pains were closer together. When they were so close that the baby might well have flown right out of her, she decided it was time to go. However, little Erik had other plans and was not ready to be born so easily. In fact, the cord was wrapped around his neck a couple of times, which made it impossible for Marie to push him out. If she tried, he would likely have choked and died. She explained how the doctors tied her legs onto the stirrups and nurses held onto each of her hands. When her body wanted to push she had to resist until the cord could be cut. When she finally pushed him out his body looked limp and white as a sheet, and he did not cry.

Marie also told her daughter about her easiest delivery. Jessica was the smallest baby at 6 pounds, 4 ounces. She explained that the doctor had her sit up and draw her knees to her chest. While she held them with her hands she took deep breaths and pushed. After a couple of good pushes the baby shot out and the doctor caught her like a baseball in a glove. Marie also explained that some babies were just more difficult to deliver than others depending on their size and the circumstances.

"Either way," Marie said, "...it will be something you never forget. It will be one day of pain you have to endure dear, but once you see the baby, you'll forget all about the pain you felt."

Jacy had also undergone drastic life changes since Jenny moved to Oklahoma. He had no idea that he would look at life so differently - like peering through a new pair of glasses. He never expected to fall in love either, and did not care who knew it. Over time however, he realized how caring and compassionate Jenny was, and wanted to be with her – and their baby – for the rest of his life. He did not care that they had to wait until after they graduated to marry, and knew he would need to get a job to take care of them. His pot smoking, drinking days were definitely over and he was more than happy about that.

Sometimes Jacy wondered what kind of story he would tell his future child about how he and mommy met. He recalled the night they made love, and he discovered that she was a virgin. Although he wanted to have sex again, the following night he just cuddled her. He had feelings for her back then, but would never have admitted it.

During birthing classes Jacy enjoyed helping Jenny with her breathing exercises, and felt he could play a useful part in the baby's delivery. He was thrilled to see the ultra sound some months before, and thought he might have seen a little boy part but said nothing. Although he eagerly looked forward to the baby's birth, like Jenny, the idea of it actually happening scared him too.

§

January arrived and the children's first day back to school was exceptionally cold. Erik, Jessica and Regina complained as they dragged themselves out the door. One thing about Oklahoma was that the weather could change from day to day, warming up just as fast as a cold front set in.

With the festivities of the holidays and the baby shower over, Jenny grew easily bored again. It did not help that Jacy was back to school as well. His visits had to wait until the end of each school day. However, she was happy that he decided not to skip school or take drugs anymore. He told her that he knew he had to be more responsible. After all, he was going to father a baby from the most beautiful girl in school he said, and he wanted to make her proud.

In the meantime, Jenny knew she needed to keep

herself busy with schoolwork, and again looked forward to the days when her teacher dropped by. Rubbing her eyes, she tried to refocus on her reading. Since she could not sit or lie down comfortably for any length of time, it was particularly distracting.

Near the end of January as she waited for her teacher to arrive, she noticed pangs of pain in her abdomen. It was below her belly button and lasted for about five minutes before subsiding. She went to the bathroom and realized that she had released a little blood. Initially frightened, she remembered her doctor's words…

"Blood vessels can burst, so don't worry unless you start bleeding severely."

Her teacher showed up and they settled in at the kitchen table. She used a pillow to sit on while the teacher explained what she needed to know to graduate. The teacher also reminded Jenny that six weeks after the baby was born she could return to school, something she hoped to do. As the teacher continued her studies Jenny felt another strong pain. She hugged her stomach and winced.

"Is everything all right?" The teacher asked.

"I'm fine," she said, attempting to reassure both herself and the teacher. "It's just a little pain." She paused for a moment and tried to relax.

"I was told that sometimes you could have what they call Braxton Hicks or false labor."

Although she tried to ignore the pangs it clearly showed on her face. Taking a helpful approach, her teacher coached her on her breathing until it subsided.

"It stopped," Jenny said with a sigh of relief, and rubbed her stomach in little circles. "Not yet, little one," she laughed noting that she was thirty-five weeks along. "It isn't time yet."

Fortunately the pain did not come back, and she was able to finish her schoolwork. After the teacher left she sat next to the picture window in the living room, and patiently waited for Jacy. When she spotted his truck she rushed to the door to greet him. After what she experienced earlier, she desperately wanted a hug from Jacy to make her feel more at ease.

They sat on the couch while he talked about school, the tests he took, and how proud he was that he'd passed them. Then they discussed their baby, and what name they might choose. She did not tell him about the pain or the spotting of blood because she wanted to avoid making him worry.

The weekend went by without further incident, and Friday night was enjoyed as usual. She had not spotted anymore and the pressure in her abdomen was gone so she believed it was nothing to be concerned about.

The following Monday morning Jenny felt a little strange as she dragged her feet to the bathroom. She could not put her finger on it, but she felt rather dizzy. She forced herself to wash her face, and brush her teeth and hair before going back to lie down for a while. She did not know how long she slept, but awoke in terrible agony. It felt like a knife ripping right through her. She tried to get up but the pain was unbearable. After it stopped for what seemed like seconds, it returned with even more intensity. Then she felt a warm sensation. Pushing against the headboard she managed to sit up, but the room started to spin. She closed her eyes tightly hoping it would stop. When it didn't, she slid her legs along the sheets toward the floor. The pain eased for another few moments and returned so violently that it brought tears to her eyes. She knew she needed help.

"Mom!" She screamed. Jenny pushed the covers off her body to see her abdomen. It was covered in blood.

Immediately, her heart beat faster and she shook uncontrollably.

"My baby!" She screeched. "Mom, I need you!"

Marie heard her chilling scream and ran to her room. When she entered she was so gripped with fear that her heart leapt up to her throat. She saw her daughter clinging to a small table next to the bed – her tummy soaked with blood and tears streaming down her face. She quickly moved toward her and helped her stand up.

"Mom," she sobbed, "my baby!"

"Don't worry, honey. Everything will be all right."

Jenny's legs wobbled as Marie helped her into the bathroom. She sat her on the toilet and helped her clean up. Then she ran back to her daughter's room to find some clean dry clothes. All the while, Jenny sobbed so hard it was difficult for her to catch her breath. She did not understand what was happening and wanted the pain to stop.

"It hurts so much, mom," she gasped.

"Breath slowly, Jenny," Marie instructed. "The baby needs you to control your breathing."

At that point Jenny was more than happy to let her mother take control. When she calmed down a little Marie helped her into the clean clothes. Then she put an arm around her for support and helped her down the stairs. Once in the kitchen, she called the doctor who advised that they get to the hospital right away. She immediately grabbed her keys and assisted Jenny outside to the car.

"What's going on, mom?" She asked as Marie tumbled into the driver's seat.

Everything was happening quickly, and the baby was not due yet. The pain and the bleeding were totally unexpected and Jenny feared for her unborn child's life.

She knew that labor pains stopped and started but this was entirely different.

"Is something wrong with my baby?" She asked anxiously. "I need to talk to Jacy. Can you call him?"

"I will when we get to the hospital."

24. A Baby Too Soon

Jacy's attention rose when the school nurse burst into his classroom with a worried expression on her face. She whispered something to his teacher before they both gazed up at him. The dire expressions on their faces caused his stomach to churn. As the nurse turned to leave, his teacher called his name sending a feeling of dread throughout his entire body.

"Jacy, please go to the office," she said attempting to remain calm.

For a moment he just sat staring at her, but when she gave him an urgent look, he jumped up and ran down the hall. His stomach felt queasy as he pushed open the office door out of breath. When the door slammed behind him, the secretary looked up.

"Jacy," she said, her eyes displaying obvious concern. "The principal wants to talk to you." She nodded toward the principal's door and Jacy followed her lead.

Inside the office, the principal's face clearly conveyed that something was terribly wrong.

"Sit down son," he urged.

"If you don't mind sir, I'd rather stand," he answered, his heart beating frantically in his chest.

"Okay," the principal said as water droplets formed on his forehead. "Now I need you to be calm."

That was the last thing Jacy could do at that point. He

rocked back and forth from foot to foot and wondered what was wrong. Perhaps his mother was hurt or something happened to his father. Time seemed to stand still while the principal carefully considered his words.

"I know you're only 16 years old son," he began, "...and you are not a relative, but I do understand your involvement."

Jacy immediately knew whom he was talking about.

"What happened to Jenny?" He demanded pacing the room. All he could hear was his own footsteps as he waited for the answer.

"She's at the hospital Jacy. I think she's having the baby."

Jacy stopped in his tracks knowing the baby was not due yet. Then anger took over and he glared at the principal.

"Excuse me, but that's *our* baby," he corrected, and turned on his heels to leave.

Jacy raced down the school hallway and the bell rang sending students rushing out of each doorway. While they attempted to get to their next class on time, Jacy pushed and shoved anyone in his way. He raced to the nearest exit and out to his truck in the parking lot. Revving the engine he sped out onto the street. The hospital was ten miles away and he knew he should slow down, but adrenalin rushed through his body, and the blood in his veins pumped so hard that it made his head hurt. Imagining the worst, he could not even think straight.

Up ahead the light was green, but Jacy saw the train coming from the left. It was a long one, and he knew he might get stuck at the tracks for fifteen minutes or more. He calculated how far away it was, and how fast he was going. The red train lights began to blink on and off. The stoplight turned red and he hit the gas pedal. He glanced to the left again and figured he could make it. He needed to get to Jenny, and a train was not going to stop him.

The truck wheels squealed as they raced ahead faster – but the train was getting closer. Jacy knew it was too late to slow down, and pressed the pedal even further. Then the truck jumped off the ground and the back wheels spun wildly. The horn ringing from the train hurt his ears. *I can do this*, he thought. *I can do this*.

All Jacy could think of was Jenny, and the child that was not ready to be born. When he reached the tracks the train slammed mercilessly into his truck and pushed it down the track. Jacy jerked forward and the force of the train pushed his head into the windshield. When he fell backward, his body fell to the right and his head hit the glass on the door. The window cracked and his head began to bleed. All his weight then fell onto the seat of the truck.

Jacy was overcome with excruciating pain in his legs, head and arm. He could not move, and thought his entire body was being crushed. Metal was bent and glass shattered. The scraping of the train's wheels being pushed along the tracks was like someone running their nails along a chalkboard, but a thousand times louder. It was the last thing he heard before he passed out.

Just an hour earlier Marie drove down Main Street much faster than she normally would, and even went through yellow lights, but she got Jenny to the hospital safely. She walked her into the emergency room where a nurse had a wheelchair waiting for them. She took them into an examining room and arranged for them to see a staff obstetrician. Even though Marie had cleaned her daughter up and put a pad on her, her clothes were drenched in blood again.

"How long has this been going on?" The nurse asked somewhat distressed.

"Just a little while ago," Marie replied. "When she got up from a nap she told me about the pain, and then I saw the blood. I cleaned her up, called the doctor, and here we are."

"Are you still in pain, young lady?" She asked, as they left the room and moved down a hospital hallway. The nurse walked quickly pushing the wheelchair and Marie tried to keep up.

"Yes," Jenny cried, hot tears staining her face.

Every time the pain returned she grabbed her mother's hand, squeezed and practiced her breathing. Marie wanted to cry too, but knew she had to be strong in front of her daughter. She was practically running alongside the nurse and the wheel chair. Then Dr. Sparks appeared and met them in the hall. Dressed in scrubs and ready to work, she pointed to a room for them to enter.

"It's going to be okay Jenny," Dr. Sparks said as she observed her.

The teen's frightened look and the red soiled clothes left an impression that things were bad, so the doctor knew she had to work fast with Jenny's co-operation.

"I want you to let the nurse help you change into a hospital gown now," she said gently but firmly.

"Can my mom stay in here with me?" Jenny asked.

The doctor nodded affirmative, and with Marie's help the nurse got her cleaned up again and into a fresh gown. Jenny climbed carefully onto the bed and a fetal monitor was placed on her belly. The monitor took her vitals and listened to the baby's heartbeat. Jenny desperately needed to hear that heartbeat, because she could not remember feeling the baby move that day. The doctor then decided to palpate her tummy to determine the baby's position in the womb.

"Put your feet into these stirrups please, Jenny," she said softly.

The doctor's pleasant and warm bedside manner helped everyone relax. She put on surgical gloves and felt between Jenny's legs.

"There has been a lot of bleeding," she said while examining her. "I don't feel the head, and you're bleeding too much." She paused to take off her bloody gloves, moved to Jenny's side to stroke her head. "Remember what I told you about placenta previa?" She asked.

Another pain started and Jenny squeezed her mother's hand unable to speak. The doctor used her wristwatch to determine that it lasted three minutes. At that point another nurse entered the room.

"The OR is ready for you now," she announced.

Jenny and Marie both shot their eyes up at the doctor.

"Doesn't OR mean operating room?" Marie asked stunned.

"You need an emergency c-section Jenny," Dr. Sparks announced. "We will take good care of you and your baby, but we have to do this now. You're bleeding too much, and we're worried about your unborn child."

Marie felt visibly weak in the knees. A feeling of nausea took over and she almost fell, but knew she had to stay strong a little bit longer for her daughter's sake. Jenny looked up at her mom with concern.

"I'm fine and so will you be, dear," Marie said convincingly.

"Are you going to call Jacy?" Jenny asked, her eyes pleading. She grabbed her mother's hand with both of hers waiting for her answer.

Marie said she'd do it immediately, but would have to leave the room. When she returned, she leaned down and kissed her daughter's forehead. Then her lips formed a smile.

"You're going to be a mama soon, young lady." As her bed rolled down the hall to the OR, she added, "I'm so proud of you." Then she said a silent prayer that everything would be all right.

"Dear Lord, please take care of my baby and my grandbaby."

25. Life & Death

The scene at the railroad tracks after the crash was pandemonium. Certainly many mothers were thinking, "Not again." Many of them had already complained about that railroad track and the death of students because of it.

The train had smashed into the left side of Jacy's truck and his body hung half way out of it. Sirens squealed and people ran around the site, which was littered with glass and metal. Two fire trucks arrived along with an ambulance, and they used the Jaws of Life to cut his body out of the vehicle. Ten firefighters worked feverishly to cut parts of the truck away until the body was freed. They were shocked to see that he was still breathing, although it was a great struggle for him.

"Quick!" The fire captain shouted. "We need the ambulance crew here now!"

The crew pulled out a stretcher, and placed Jacy's mangled body onto it. Then they placed an oxygen mask on his face, which was bruised, disfigured and covered with blood. His right arm was broken in three places. Both legs were also broken, and bent in an awkward way. They ran him quickly to the ambulance, turned on the siren and warning lights, and sped away. One medic called the hospital to let the medical team know they would be there any minute with yet another victim who tried to race the train. Another medic took his vitals, while yet another put in IV's and the ECG monitor.

Jacy was unconscious, but looked down at himself as the fire and emergency crews tried to save his body. He wondered if he was dead. He watched as they rolled him into an emergency room, but did not feel anything when they lifted his body from the gurney onto a bed.

In the other operating room at the same hospital a doctor ordered an anesthesiologist to knock the patient out. An IV was inserted and soon sleeping syrup dripped through it. Jenny tried to stay focused and heard a couple of nurse's talking in quiet tones. The fluorescent lights glared above her face, and she could hear the dripping of the IV fluid.

"Jenny," said the doctor through a blue facemask. "You're going to sleep for a little while. Soon you'll see your baby."

Jenny tried to acknowledge her with a smile, but was experiencing double vision of two Dr. Sparks. She was not sure which one was talking to her, and did not comprehend what she said.

"Goodbye baby," she said as she drifted into unconsciousness.

Jacy seemed to fly into the room and saw Jenny lying on a table unconscious. He watched as a team of nurses and technicians worked on her – one putting on monitor leads and another inserting an IV. Then they cut open her belly and he saw his baby.

Just as suddenly- he flew back to the OR, where doctors worked feverishly to save his life.

"He isn't breathing," someone said.

A technician began chest compressions, while another placed a bag valve mask on him and began administering oxygen. Then a doctor walked into the busy room.

"He's in V-tac!" A nurse yelled.

The doctor turned on the monitor and let the electricity run through it.

"Clear! Clear! Clear!" He yelled three times before releasing electricity into his body.

Jacy watched as his body jumped up off the bed and then back down again. Everyone waited quietly, but nothing happened.

"Give him some Epinephrine. You, CPR please while I increase the jewels," ordered the doctor.

Quickly they administered the drug while another technician performed CPR until the doctor told him to stop.

"Clear! Clear! Clear!" he shouted before shocking the body again. The body jumped for a second time and fell back on the bed. Everyone stared in silence at the monitor on the wall.

"A-systole," yelled a nurse.

Quickly the two techs began chest compressions and oxygen again, as the doctor gave him more Epinephrine. Then he looked at the monitor to see if the drug was having any effect.

"Stop!" He hollered.

The monitor still showed a flat line. Sadly he turned to his staff and said, "We lost him."

In the other OR, the doctor and nurses monitored Jenny's vitals and a cardiac monitor. She had lost a lot of blood, and the baby was in great distress. Jenny's pulse slipped down to a dangerous level, and her blood pressure dropped. They had to work quickly to open her abdomen.

When they removed the little living being it did not cry. They quickly put her in an incubator and took her to the nursery.

Meanwhile, Jenny's blood pressure continued drop and Dr. Sparks was afraid she would go into shock.

"Put in another IV," she demanded while she worked to sew her back up. "Jenny, stay with us."

When the doctor was finished, Jenny was wheeled to her room with two IV's running, one with medication and one with blood. She was then put on oxygen and the legs of the bed were raised.

Jim found Marie sitting in the hospital waiting room with a Kleenex covering her face. A few other people sat talking so she never heard him walk up, but she did recognize the arms that went around her shoulders to comfort her, and the voice that gently whispered in her ear, "I'm here, honey."

Marie stood up when he came to her, clung to his neck and sobbed uncontrollably. Jim felt her body shake, and wished he had been home to drive them to the hospital.

"I've been praying," she cried. "Do you think we're being punished?"

She held him tighter and he could feel his throat swell up inside. He did not want his tears to show, so he could be strong for her.

"No, dear," he whispered. "God doesn't work that way."

Dr. Sparks found the two of them holding onto each other.

"Marie, Jim?" She said quietly.

They immediately parted to greet her.

"Can we talk?"

Her words sent a chill through Marie and she gasped

aloud. Jim quickly grabbed her hands.

"First, you have a healthy granddaughter," she smiled, which helped to ease their stress.

"So the baby is doing well?" Marie asked as she dropped into a nearby chair. "Thank you, God."

"Yes but there's more. Jim, you may want to sit down too."

He slid into the chair next to Marie, but kept his eyes on the doctor. He was afraid of what she might say next. Dr. Sparks pulled up a chair across from them and sat as well.

"At the moment your daughter is in critical condition," she said, her eyes displaying the pain she felt about sharing this news. "Her blood pressure is quite low. She has lost a lot of blood and we're doing everything we can right now."

"No!" Marie cried shaking her head. "She has to be fine. She has a baby to take care of." Sobbing again and struggling for air she added, "She's worked so hard to finish high school and to learn about babies. Between Jenny and Jacy, that baby would have a good start."

Marie turned to Jim and then upward, her eyes pleading and a hand over her mouth. "Please God, let her be all right," she begged.

The doctor took Marie's hand and tried to rub the crease from her forehead. Denial was always the initial result whenever she had to deliver bad news… but that was not all.

"There's more," she interjected, her throat tightening.

Marie and Jim looked at each other with dread. *What else could possibly be wrong?* Marie wondered.

"It's about Jacy," Dr. Sparks began, her voice cracking.

Jenny and Jacy had become inseparable. He had

accompanied her to all her appointments, and Dr. Sparks could see how vested he was in their relationship, as well as their soon-to-be baby. This was the hardest part of her job and she took a deep breath before she continued.

"Jacy was involved in an accident today. He tried to outrun a train, but didn't make it."

"No, God, no!" Marie wailed.

Jim grabbed her and let her cry into his chest. Then he glanced up at Doctor Sparks.

"Thank you, doctor," he whispered and turned his attention back to his wife.

Dr. Sparks stood up, but before turning to leave she said, "I'm so sorry for your loss. On the positive side, you should be able to see your granddaughter very soon."

Marie cried until she had no more tears left to shed. She could not believe that Jacy would never set eyes on his baby. He would never get to touch the child, or experience her first step. He would not be there for Jenny. He would not take her to her prom, or help her raise their child. Marie recalled her initial dislike for Jacy in the beginning, and how Jenny's love for him caused her to reconsider.

Marie pushed away from Jim and sat up straight to face him. The lines under his eyes showed he was crying inside. She touched his brow, slowly moving her hands down his cheek to his lips. Then he kissed her fingers and placed them on his mouth.

"I love you," she whispered.

Jim did not respond but his eyes conveyed his gratitude. Then Marie bowed her head.

"Dear Lord," she prayed. "I know you took Jacy home to be with you, but please Lord, let Jenny come back to us. Her baby needs her."

She was quiet for a few moments and sat with her eyes

closed. Then a small smile formed on her lips, she opened her eyes and turned to Jim.

"I want to see our grandbaby," she said rising from her chair. "Let's go ask if we can see the baby now."

As they knocked on the nursery window, Jim and Marie pointed to their grandchild who slept in a little crib. A nurse rolled the bassinette to the window so they could get a closer look. It was a baby girl and she was beautiful. She had a full head of dark hair creeping under the pink hat they put on her. She looked so small, and slept so peacefully - not a care in the world.

The nurses snuck them into the nursery, and let them hold her. As Marie cuddled the infant in her arms she cried tears of sorrow for Jacy, tears of fear for her daughter, and happiness for her new grandchild. Little did this precious new little life realize that her father had died, and her mother clung to life just on the other side of the veil.

§

Jenny did not know where she was, but an immense feeling of love, peace, and joy penetrated her being. She felt consumed by pure happiness and when she sat up, she felt no pain. Her room seemed peaceful and quiet, with no IV poles or nurses rushing in and out.

Is this what death feels like? She wondered. Slipping from under the covers, she walked out of her room and down the hall where she could hear a baby crying. She followed the sound until she found a room with the door closed. Slowly she opened it, and was surrounded with intense white light. In the middle of the light she spotted the silhouette of a man with a baby in his arms. Hesitantly she tiptoed in.

"Isn't she beautiful?" Jacy asked.

The bright light made it difficult for her eyes to focus, but as she drew near to the man he extended his arm and beckoned her to come closer. When she reached his side he put an arm on her shoulder, and it felt good - something she needed just then. She stared at his face and watched him intently as he smile down at the baby.

"I can't believe we did this," he said leaning in to kiss her lips. A sense of pure happiness seemed to envelope them.

"What do you want to name her?" He asked calmly. "The name Janie comes to my mind."

They had talked about names, but never really agreed on one, and it was strange because Janie was never one that they considered.

"How did you come up with that name?" Jenny asked.

Jacy looked down at the baby and let her tiny fingers wrap around one of his.

"Well, your name is Jenny and mine is Jacy. Both start with the letter J," he explained. "Janie just seems right."

They stood in the glory of the shining light and held each other. As they stared at their baby Jenny felt as if she never wanted to leave.

26. Facing Reality

Kristina knocked on her parents' bedroom door while the aroma of fresh brewed coffee filled the house.

"Mom, dad, its seven o'clock," she shouted. "Time to get up."

Marie rustled in the sheets next to Jim who still slept soundly. She had called Kristina the day before to ask her to wake them, so they could get an early start to the hospital. She also asked her to make dinner for her siblings, and get them off to bed.

When they left the hospital, Jenny was in a deep sleep and would not wake up. Her blood pressure was still very low. Since she had RH Negative blood, she was given a liter of it, as well as a shot of RH immune globulin. After further testing they would decide if she needed more. The nurses told Jim and Marie that they would keep an eye on their daughter, and that they should go home to get some sleep. There was really nothing they could do, but they did need to keep up their strength.

Kristina had heard their car roll up just before midnight. They strolled in wearily, and she could not help noticing the huge dark circles around their eyes. She knew they'd been through a terrible day at the hospital. When the bedroom door finally opened, Kristina ran up to them.

"Well how is she?" She asked, but her parents simply shook their heads as if to say, "We don't know anything yet."

When Marie walked into the kitchen she noticed a newspaper lying on the table. The front page featured a picture of a train hooked onto the side of a mangled familiar looking pickup truck. She grabbed a cup and poured her morning get-up-and-go coffee. She then sat at the table and picked up the paper. Horror struck her heart as she read what happened:

At 2 p.m. the pickup truck bolted with the train across the tracks. It was said by bystanders that the truck accelerated when he noticed the train getting closer. This is another tragedy of a high school teenager racing the train. Mothers of the students at Richards High have been protesting that too many children have already died trying to beat the train, and school lunches should be kept on campus.

Tears filled Marie's eyes as she tried to keep reading. It was particularly difficult to learn that Jacy tried to beat the train, even though the newspaper had it wrong. He was not trying to beat the train after lunch like other students who met his fate. He was rushing to his girl who was having his baby. Her body slumped over the table and she rested her head on her hands. So much had happened in such a small period of time that she could hardly take it all in. At the same time she was terribly worried about Jenny. The hospital did not call, so she figured her daughter must still be asleep. Just the thought of another death – especially of her own flesh and blood – terrified her.

Marie had no idea how she could tell Jenny about Jacy's death. With that thought, her body involuntarily shivered. She desperately needed to dredge up a happy thought, so she turned her mind toward her new and precious granddaughter. The baby would be the saving grace to get her through this distressing time, and keep her motivated when all else failed.

Jim strolled into the kitchen dressed for the day, but his hair was still wet from the shower. "Morning" he said pouring a cup of coffee.

Marie continued to stare at the picture in the newspaper. Jim sat down and gave her a quick kiss on the forehead. She glanced up at him and tried to smile, but he could see the tracks of tears on her face again. When she passed him the paper his eyes opened wide. Then they sat in silence as he read the article. Marie stared out the kitchen window. After about fifteen minutes she got up to take her shower so they could get to the hospital.

Along the way they passed the high school and saw people surrounding the building with picket signs. Some of the signs portrayed photographs of teenagers who had been killed by the train. Too many students had died, and they wanted to finally put an end to it. Either the kids stay in school for lunch or the train should not run during school hours, they insisted. They loudly chanted the same thing over and over again: "Save our kids."

Mothers and fathers, grandmothers and grandfathers stood outside shouting. Mrs. Everstein and her husband stood with the group holding a picture of Stephen. Some students also decided to take part. Marie remembered the meeting in which the students were against the idea.

What changed their minds? She wondered. Scanning through the crowd she recognized a small group of kids standing in the corner holding signs. They looked like the kids that were at Jenny's birthday party, she recalled. When she strained her eyes to see what their signs said, she recognized a picture of Jacy, and chills raced down her spine.

Upon arriving at the hospital, they went straight to the nursery to see their new grandbaby. They spent some time holding the infant, and then went to Jenny's room. When they entered her eyes were closed, but she let out a small moan. Since this was the first response they'd seen from her, Marie could not help getting excited.

"Jenny, sweetie?" She whispered as she caressed her face. "Are you awake?"

Jim ran out of the room to get the nurse while Marie visually examined her daughter. Two bags of fluid hung above her with tubes going into her arms. One was filled with blood so she knew her labs were taken again and her blood was still low. Someone had combed the front of her hair letting it cascade over her shoulders, but she had tubes going into her nose with oxygen running through them. Jenny's body seemed so terrifyingly helpless.

"Good morning," said the nurse entering the room. She moved to Jenny's bedside and took her vitals.

"I heard her moaning," Marie interjected.

The nurse just shook her head as she finished her job.

"Good," she finally said. "Her blood pressure is up. I think the moaning is a good sign. Hopefully, this means she will be coming around soon."

"Thank you God," quickly escaped Marie's lips.

The nurse carefully lifted the covers to expose Jenny's belly. Marie could not bear to see the stitches on her abdomen. The nurse pressed on her stomach, and then neatly put the covers over her again. She smiled at Marie and Jim as she left the room.

"Thank you," Marie called out behind her.

Around noon Jenny began to wake up. She slowly

opened her eyes and tried to focus, but everything seemed blurry. She closed them again thinking about the place she last saw Jacy and her baby daughter. How peaceful it had been. She knew she needed to be with her baby again. When she fully opened her eyes, she saw two figures staring down at her, but could not distinguish their faces. She could feel some pain in her belly and an annoying tube in her nose. Unfortunately, the feeling of happiness she felt before had vanished.

"Jenny?" Marie cried leaning over to kiss her forehead. "We were so worried about you."

Jim took his daughter's hand, squeezed it and smiled gratefully. The idea of losing one of his children was too much to bear and for the first time, he could not contain his tears.

"Where are Jacy and Janie?" Jenny whispered.

"Who's Janie?" Marie asked thinking her child might be hallucinating. She quickly shot a terrified look toward her husband.

"My baby, of course," she said sincerely. "I was with her and Jacy last night. She's so beautiful."

Marie scanned her daughter's face curiously. *How was that possible?* She wondered. She never woke up when she had her baby, and Jacy had died. Marie tried to fight the tears that now blistered in her eyes.

"Jenny," she said, her voice shaking. "There's something I have to tell you." Jenny looked at mother confused.

"You lost a lot of blood when you had your baby yesterday, and your blood pressure dropped. You were in serious condition and we weren't sure you would make it."

Jenny squinted and tried to understand. However, she did notice that her mother looked tired.

"They had you on a lot of medication that could have caused you to see things that weren't real."

"I didn't hallucinate, mom. We were together last night in one of these rooms, and the light was so bright. I saw them both."

Marie clasped her daughter's hand and prayed silently for a moment. "Thank you God for giving her back to us. Now please help her understand."

Jenny smiled widely as she continued to explain what she experienced.

"Jacy was holding our baby when I walked into the room. He put his arm around me and kissed me. He told me to call her Janie."

She watched as her mother shook her head, and could feel her squeeze tighten up. Tears welled in her eyes, and her body began to shake. She could not comprehend why her mother did not believe her, and her imagination took over.

"Where's my baby?" She cried her eyes wide with fear. "Did something happen to my baby?" She broke into a deep and heartfelt sob, so her parents moved to each side of her bed and held onto her.

"Shh, shh," Marie soothed. "Everything's all right."

"Your baby is healthy and happy, Jenny," her father whispered. "I'll tell the nurse to bring her in if you like?"

"And Jacy?" She sniffed. "I want to see him too."

Marie and Jim glanced at each other. They knew she had to know, but how? Jim left the room while Marie stayed by her side.

Courage, Marie told herself. "Please God give me the strength."

"Jacy isn't here, sweetie," Marie said in a low voice.

Jenny raised her eyes to her mother questioningly and

Marie took her hand again.

"Jacy tried to get here before you had the baby."

"I know," Jenny interrupted. "I was with him." When Marie diverted her eyes for a second she added, "What is it mom?"

"He wanted to get here so fast," Marie continued trying not to break down. "He tried to beat the train by the school, but he didn't make it."

For a few moments Jenny did not respond. She was unable to take in her mother's words because she could not imagine losing Jacy. When she finally realized what had occurred she cried out "No!" Her arms flew into the air almost pulling out the IV's.

"No! That's not true, mom. I saw him," she wailed.

Marie leaned in close to her daughter and held her tight as she sobbed uncontrollably. It seemed like an eternity before the dire mood was broken. Jim entered the room and Jenny heard what sounded like a kitten crying. He pushed a bassinette beside the bed so she could see the infant inside.

"Someone's hungry," he noted wistfully.

Jenny peered down at the infant and wiped the tears from her face. She asked Marie to pass the baby to her. As she held her newborn child her face softened and she could not help smiling.

"I'm your mother, Janie," she said holding her close to take in her sweet scent. When she looked into her baby's eyes she felt a huge lump in her throat. They were just like Jacy's. Instinctively, she rocked the baby and softly sang her a lullaby.

27. Reality Sets In

Jessica and Regina finished putting up the last of the balloons on either side of the banner that hung on the wall in Jenny's room. Excitement filled the air as they pulled fresh sheets across her bed and tucked them in. Erik and Jim had the crib put together and hung a colorful mobile at one end. Some new stuffed animals sat inside. It seemed rather odd with half of the room looking like a nursery and the other like that of a teenager, but it was the best they could do. Jessica and Regina turned on the mobile so they could hear the melody and watch it spin.

"They're here!" Kristina shouted when she heard the car enter the driveway. Everyone ran outside. Amidst the throng of children, Jim carefully lifted the baby's car seat from the back seat. Once inside the house seven sets of eyes peered at the sleeping infant.

"Hi Janie," Regina said with enthusiasm. "You're home!"

The baby continued to sleep as Jenny passed her around so everyone could hold and kiss her. But after all the excitement was over and everyone went to bed, she had Janie all to herself. She sat in a chair in her bedroom and rocked her new daughter.

Over the next few weeks Jenny wavered between joy over the baby, and agony over Jacy's death. Finally her mood swings led to deep depression. Her 17th birthday came and went without cheering her up, and life seemed like a never-ending job of changing diapers, preparing bottles, and feeding the baby. The hardest part was when the baby cried for hours on end. Jenny tried to console her but sometimes it seemed that the baby felt her mother's distressed emotions and would not settle down.

Jenny's siblings stepped in to help whenever they could. Kristina sometimes sang to Janie in her operatic voice until she drifted off. Other times Erik took the baby into his room and played the song Hazard by Richard Marx over and over again. Even though the music blared, it took only about fifteen minutes for him to emerge with a sleeping baby in his arms. Jenny could not believe it! Of course Marie had the touch and knew how to sway with Janie to put her to sleep, but she was not always around.

The house became a holding place for diapers, blankets, and sleepers strewn on couches and chairs, but since everyone became involved in the baby's life, no one cared. Janie was the main focus of all the attention - the center of their universe. She brought such joy to Jenny's life, but her world continued to spiral out of control.

Jenny had little time to herself, so she could not properly mourn Jacy's death. His father had his funeral on the reservation while she was still in the hospital. She missed him so much and still could not comprehend how she saw him holding their baby. She wondered if she might have been dreaming, or perhaps having a near death experience. Either way she felt lost, confused, scared and barely able to hold on. Yet she had a small human life that depended on her and as a mother, and she knew the baby must come first. Lacking in sleep and progressively more depressed, Jenny soon felt tired all over. However, she thanked God that her family was there to help her.

When Janie turned six weeks old, Jenny's home schooling ended. She had to go back to the high school, but felt insecure and unprepared. On her first day back she awoke earlier than usual and was glad she did. Janie took more of her bottle and needed an extra diaper change. She put diapers, bottles, formula, extra baby clothes, and pacifiers into a diaper bag before heading out.

Jenny secured Janie in her car seat and fastened her seat belt in the big yellow 1976 Buick LeSabre her father had bought for her. She hated the old automobile, but he said she needed a sturdy vehicle to get to school in with her baby. Even though driving the car felt like steering a boat, Jim felt the larger, stronger vehicle would be much safer for his daughter and grandchild.

Jenny drove to the school nursery first and felt a lump form in her throat as she brought her baby girl inside. She did not feel comfortable leaving her there – something she never expected, but she had not left her side since the day she was born.

"Janie will be fine," said Lynn, as she put another sleeping baby into a crib. Lynn had been there herself, and understood Jenny's concern.

"How have you been?" She asked offering a hug.

"Good." Jenny picked her baby up from the car seat and brought her to her face. "Babies smell so good, don't they?"

"I think it's the lotion and the powder," Lynn giggled. "She's beautiful. Can I hold her?"

Jenny hugged her baby one more time before handing her over.

"I have to go to class," she said dropping the diaper bag on top of the car seat. "I'll be back during fourth period. Here's the list of classes and teachers just in case you need me."

She placed the sheet of paper on the board with those of others. Then she rushed back, kissed her baby and waved goodbye.

"She's in good hands," Lynn assured. "Don't worry."

Jenny rushed out of the building with an anxious ball of energy swelling up inside of her. She had to stop and catch her breath. Her heart pounded out of her chest, while she struggled to slow her breathing down. She could not believe how her body reacted, and wondered if it was stress-related because she had to leave her baby. Even if it was, she knew getting her high school diploma was vitally important if she expected to be able to support her.

The dream of having a family with Jacy would never be realized, so Jenny knew she needed to find her own way in the world. When she first told her mother that she was expecting, Marie made her promise to finish high school. She considered night school, but her mother advised that if she put it off and did not finish school at that time, she might never acquire her diploma. She would always find something else hindering her progress, and might one day blame her child for not succeeding.

It seemed like a lifetime since Jenny heard the slamming of lockers, and rustling of teenagers pushing and shoving through the hallways. She now wore a different pair of eyes, and had an alternative mindset. *I am now an adult*, she thought.

She had responsibilities and for her child's sake, she needed to finish what she had started. Jenny heard some kids gossiping and giggling, and saw others walking hand-in-hand. So much had happened… and changed since she'd last walked those halls. In the process, she learned the lessons and consequences that result from playing adult games. There was no turning back and even if she could, she was not sure she would want it.

For a moment Jenny longed to be an innocent junior again, meeting a boy for a date, and wondering if he liked her. However, seeing her baby later that day would quickly dissipate those thoughts. She was back to reality. While she helped change diapers and feed some of the babies, she realized just how dependent they were on those who took care of them. She also understood that they did not ask to be born, and deserved so much. She knew Janie needed her more than anyone, and finishing school would help her take care of her in the best way possible.

That morning as she walked the hall, a couple of teens stopped in their tracks and gawked at her.

"Sorry, Jenny," they said in unison and offered a half smile.

How odd, she thought. *Do I even know them?*

Then another girl stopped and touched her on the shoulder. "Sorry, Jenny," she echoed with a painful frown.

What's going on? She wondered.

Continuing down the hall a few more people stopped her and said they were sorry. When she reached her locker she spotted a picture taped to it, and her heart jumped. It was from the newspaper and showed a train rammed into a pickup truck. Below the words were: "You will be missed, Jacy," and under that said, "We are sorry, Jenny," written so neatly.

Suddenly she felt flushed, and tears filled her eyes. Her heart beat faster, and chills ran up and down her arms. She stood wringing her hands while reading and re-reading the front of her locker. She hadn't had time to mourn, and it finally was hitting her. Her throat became dry making it hurt to swallow. She thought she had everything under control, but then without warning, she was losing it.

Trying to focus through the tears, she noticed some of the other lockers had the same picture taped to them. She had been told about the accident, but seeing the picture finally made it real. Jenny began to tremble. The room started to spin and she grabbed onto her locker. Some kids passed by mumbling something about being sorry, but she could not grasp their words. The room seemed to revolve faster and faster. Her body felt weak and then everything turned black. The next thing she knew, a pair of strong hands helped her down to the floor.

"Are you all right Jenny?" A girl's voice said.

"Jenny!" A boy's voice yelled. "Wake up!" He shook her but got no response. "Quick, go get the nurse," he hollered.

A small crowd gathered around making it difficult for Amanda and the nurse to squeeze their way through. Gary held Jenny's head in his lap. The nurse put some smelling salts under her nose and she woke up. When she opened her eyes she saw an angel in white leaning over her.

"What happened?" She asked with embarrassment.

Gary's strong arms still held her. The nurse bent over and Gary put an arm around Jenny's waist to help her up.

"Are you okay?" The nurse asked.

Just then the bell rang sending students running for their classes.

"She didn't fall," Gary volunteered. "Amanda and I passed her in the hall and tried to talk to her, but she didn't say anything back so I turned around and noticed her hugging the lockers before she started to go down. When I ran up to her, she started to faint so I grabbed her and sat down with her."

Jenny stood weaving back and forth from one foot to

the other. She could feel her face turn red and stared at the floor.

"How do you feel now, young lady?" The nurse asked with concern. "Do you want to sit the next period out in the nurse office with me?"

When she shook her head no, Gary said he would walk with her to make sure she did not fall again. But her legs wobbled and before she knew what happened, she found herself lying on a bed in the nurses' room.

"It's okay, honey," the nurse soothed. "You're in shock. You've gone through a lot for a girl your age."

The nurse turned off the light, and it gave Jenny time to take a nap and reflect. Jenny waited until all was quiet before allowing a flood of tears and the severity of her loss to consume her. She thought of Jacy and her hand automatically touched the silver locket around her neck. She missed him more than she could ever say. She longed for his touch, his kiss - even just his presence around her. She let out a loud sob by accident and grabbed the pillow to muffle her cries. Her chest hurt, but not with the kind of pain any medicine could heal. Her heart was broken.

Why? Why did he have to try and outrun the train? She questioned.

She hated that train, and decided that if she did anything in her life, she would find a way to either get rid of the tracks or have a bridge built over them so no one would die again. She continued to cry until no more tears fell.

"God, am I being punished?" she whispered. "Why did you take Jacy away from me?" Then exhausted, she fell asleep.

At the beginning of her fourth hour a light flashed on and she quickly sat up rubbing her red and swollen eyes.

The school nurse stood at the doorway and could see the dark lines under her eyes.

"Jenny," she said, "I talked to the principal and we both agreed that you should go home for the rest of the day."

Jenny quickly jumped off the bed.

"Thank you," she said and ran out to her locker.

She put in her books and then headed to the nursery to get her baby. She needed to see Janie. She had Jacy's eyes, and that was the closest thing she could get her hands on to be near him again.

28. Life Goes On

With the renewal of spring, flowers blossomed in a burst of colors, and the trees turned green again. With the warmer days, Jenny was able to take Janie out in her buggy. One day she went for a walk with Marie and Erik. Stretching her legs and feeling the wind on her face seemed so refreshing. She did not want to think of the past anymore. She realized that all her wishing and crying would never bring Jacy back. She had to concentrate on the future and her wonderful baby. She did not want her child to grow up without a father, but no one could ask for more support than her family had shown. They took her in with loving arms, with no talk of consequence - just acceptance and love.

As they walked a car drove up the street and honked to get their attention. It drove into the driveway and a lady stepped out. Jenny thought she recognized the driver.

"Be right back," she said turning the buggy around.

"Hi, Jenny," the woman said, her face drawn and pale.

"Hi, Mrs. Kavi."

"I just dropped by to take a peek at my granddaughter."

Jenny picked up her baby and passed her to Mrs. Kavi. As she looked at the baby, Jenny noticed the pain on her face.

She probably sees Jacy's eyes too, she thought.

She held the baby close and closed her eyes before a couple of tears escaped. After a moment she gave her a kiss and passed Janie back to her mother.

"Please let me be a part of her life?" Mrs. Kavi begged.

"You can come over anytime you want. You're a part of her family too."

With a faint smile, Mrs. Kavi said thank you and then got back into her car.

Over the next few months Janie grew, and her personality developed. Soon she had everyone wrapped around her little finger. Excitement filled the house whenever she clapped her hands, and then when she started to crawl. Jenny still had school and chores, but Janie was her first priority. However, it was difficult studying for tests when the baby demanded her attention. And she still had to get up in the middle of the night if the baby awoke. Sometimes she asked her mother or one of her sisters to take over for a while.

She still missed Jacy terribly and suffered severe bouts of depression. Whenever she spotted a couple of teenagers with their arms wrapped around each other in the school halls, she thought of him. It also bothered her when she saw her sisters go out with their friends with no care in the world, or when someone asked her to go to the mall and she had to push a stroller while her friends ran free. But Jenny planned to do well in school so she could go on to college. She was going to be the best she could be, especially since she had such great family support.

Before she knew it, Janie turned one year old and Marie decided to celebrate with a party. It turned into quite an affair with the guests including the school principal, the teachers, and the nurse, because they all played such a large part in helping Jenny in some way. Of course, Grandma Kavi showed up to spoil Janie too. Jenny's old friends Sandy, Susan, Amanda and Gary showed up, along with the girls from the nursery and their babies. The table was full of fruit, salads and pasta. Mickey Mouse decorations filled the house, and children screamed in delight when Marie tied a helium balloon to their arms. The place was full of hugs and chatter as old and new friends gathered for this special occasion.

After singing Happy Birthday and blowing out the candle, a little cake was put on Janie's tray. At first she simply stared at it not knowing what to do, but once Jenny put her little fingers in the frosting and up to her mouth, she dug in. Soon her face, hair, and clothing were covered in frosting and cake. The grandmothers assumed the honors of cleaning her while Jenny opened her presents. She loved the little dresses and short outfits in pretty greens and pinks.

The last gift bore Jenny's name written in big bold letters. She carefully tore off the tape and opened the package. Inside was a brown picture frame with wrapped molding encasing the newspaper article on the accident. Under the article the following words were written: "We miss you, Jacy – Sorry for your loss, Jenny." She could hardly believe it had been a full year since Jacy died and Janie was born. She desperately wanted to cry, but held off until everyone left the party. That present became one she would always treasure.

When she put Janie to bed that night, she got down on her knees to pray.

"Dear Lord," she whispered as she knelt beside her bed, "Thank you for all you have done for me. Help me to learn your compassion and be a good mother to my daughter - the gift you let Jacy give to me. Take care of Jacy and tell him I love him. Help me to teach Janie about the goodness in the world and the importance of family. In Jesus' name, Amen."

She climbed into bed and opened the silver locket around her neck. Looking at Jacy's face brought back a thousand memories - and tears. Molding into the bed sheets with her comforter around her she whispered, "I love you, Jacy."

Finally June rolled around and Jenny's dream of finishing high school was coming to fruition. While Janie sat in her crib playing with her toys, she tried to get dressed. Tried, because Janie decided she'd been in there long enough and started to fuss.

"Mom," Jenny shouted, "Would you keep an eye on Janie for me? I need to get ready." Her navy blue dress and graduation gown lay on her bed. Marie shuffled into the room and gladly picked up her granddaughter.

"Come to grandma, Janie," she grinned.

Janie threw her hands up and giggled. As Marie picked her up, she grabbed on and hugged her neck.

"Thanks, mom," Jenny said rushing to the bathroom to take a shower.

The big night had arrived and the auditorium was full of proud parents. Marie carried in Janie as her entire family found their seats. The graduates waited in another room and with a sense of achievement and relief, they helped each other with their caps and gowns. It was seven o'clock and the graduation was ready to begin. Bagpipers walked up the aisle and filled the auditorium with music. The students followed while families shouted and whistled to get their teen's attention.

After the principal led everyone in the Pledge of

Allegiance, one of the students sang the Star Spangle Banner. Then a number of people rose to speak, followed by a special commencement speech that was difficult to hear. A number of children could not settle down and there was some commotion with people walking in late and trying to find seats.

"Attention everyone," the principal hollered to get everyone's attention again. "May I introduce our special speaker today? She has had a tough road, but with her determination and spirit, the lessons she learned are inspirational." He paused for a moment and goose bumps crawled up Jenny's arms.

"May I present Jenny Federigo?"

The auditorium exploded with applause, and people screamed out her name. She walked shyly up to the podium, cleared her throat, and waited until everyone grew quiet. She did not expect such an overwhelming welcome. She felt flushed and knew her face must be turning red.

"School is just a stepping stone," she began, her heart fluttering in her chest. "We have been raised by our parents as someone special in their eyes. They had high expectations and high self-regard for us, but sometimes because of our own actions, they felt frustrated and disappointed in us. Now we students are entering the grown up world. We must know and accept our strengths and our weaknesses. We must look at ourselves honestly, and understand our passions, our skills, and our limitations. We must never give up." She paused for a second and could feel her arms shaking, so she clasped her hands to cover up her nervousness.

"You all know that I have not been the perfect student. I experimented with drugs, and now I am a mother," she said, her voice cracking. As her eyes began to water she added, "I lost someone in my life that meant more than the world to me." She wiped her tears with a Kleenex and without even thinking, reached for her locket to give her strength. "Help me, Lord," she silently pleaded.

"If it weren't for the support of my family, friends, and the school faculty, I would not be here today. I learned how important it is to have a goal - to be persistent and creative. At times it was not easy and I wanted to quit, but I prayed a lot, and I know God answered my prayers. I have never felt so strong or as confident, as I do today. Take a chance, feel it in your heart, take a leap of faith, and go for it... thank you."

As she walked from the podium and back to her seat, the students stood and clapped. Then everyone stood and did the same. Jenny could not stop the tears that streaked her face, but she smiled inside and out. She looked around, and spotted her mother and Janie. She was surprised to see the church pastor, who was also clapping and nodding his head with approval.

29. Back To Present

Finally Jenny returned from her drive. She had to get away and think for a while. She had driven past her old high school where she met Jacy so long ago, but everything seemed different.

The McDonald's had closed down when the students stayed on campus for lunch. She walked around the area where Jacy and his gang smoked and got high. There was no sign of cigarettes, and the grass was full and green. She stopped at the little house that was the nursery. It was still there, but Mrs. Smith had passed away a couple of years before, so there was a new manager.

Then she drove to the railroad tracks to look at the bridge that covered them. How she wished it were there years ago. It had not been easy raising her daughter without a father. She hated the fact that Jacy never witnessed her first steps, or was there when she started kindergarten. Now as her daughter began her teenage years, she realized how much stricter she had become. She did not want Janie to make the same mistakes she made all those years ago. Although she never moved Janie around like her parents, she was still frightened that she might fall in with the wrong crowd and take drugs, smoke, or even engage in sex due to peer pressure.

Maybe moving had nothing to do with what happened? She thought.

Either way, she knew Janie was a good girl. Her grandparents, aunts, and uncle were great role models who helped to mold her. She was probably the most loved child in a single mom family. Yet she still feared for her.

Perhaps worry is just part of a mother's life, she mused.

Jenny had to think it through. She wanted to keep Janie on the right path, but she did not want to push her into any situation simply because she was an overbearing parent. Walking back into the house, she caught a whiff of hamburgers on the grill. She stopped at the entrance to the kitchen and stared at the picture on the wall. It was the original article in the paper the day after Jacy died – the one that was given to her when Janie turned 1 year old. She saw the truck smashed by the train and reread the article. It seemed so long ago. She remembered how she felt giving birth that day and waiting for Jacy to show up. Then she recalled the total devastation she felt when she realized that she would never see him again. She never forgot her dream - the one where she and Jacy stood holding their new born and naming her. Under the article she reread the note from the kids at school that was put on her locker. "We Miss You, Jacy. We Are Sorry, Jenny." Whenever she read those words, tears filled her eyes again.

"I miss you, Jacy," she whispered, kissed two fingers and placed them gently on the glass.

When Jenny walked into the kitchen, she saw streamers on the walls with balloons hanging over the table. As usual, Marie always tried to make birthdays special. Regina and Jessica sat around the table talking with Marie and holding their little ones. Regina had a 9-month-old son named Paul, and Jessica a 1-year-old, Oliver.

"Everything all right?" Marie asked.

Jenny nodded, strode toward Regina and took the baby out of her hands. In her head, Regina would always be her little sister, not a mother.

"Hey, little one," she said kissing his cheek. "You happy to see your Aunt Jenny?"

Regina leaned over to give Jenny a hug. After giving her back the baby, she reached for Oliver. Jessica gave her a kiss as she gave him up to her.

"You okay, Jenny?" She asked.

Oliver reached up and wrapped his arms around her neck. She did not answer their questions, but drew the baby close taking in his scent and reminiscing.

"I love his little hugs," she said giving him a peck on his cheeks. "I remember when Janie was this small."

She gave him a few belly blows before passing him back to Jessica.

"I remember you being small too, but I was young then," Jenny giggled. "I used to get jealous of all the attention you took away from me."

They all laughed and turned to look as the front door opened. In came Kristina with her three children. She was holding Lillian, the youngest one. Damien and Madilynn ran toward any aunt who would give them a hug. Then Jenny realized that Janie was not there.

"She's still upstairs," Marie said reading her mind.

With a quick glance of thanks, Jenny crept up the stairway. She had so many memories of tiptoeing up those stairs, but for all the wrong reasons. Her daughter was in her old room and when she reached it, she saw her sleeping with a book lying on her chest. She paused at the door and looked around the room. At one time her bed and a crib were in the room. She lived a lifetime there, and had so many memories that formed her into the woman she was now.

She looks just like me at that age, Jenny thought.

She tiptoed into the room and carefully removed the book from her chest. Then she sat next to her and the movement of the bed woke Janie up.

"Hi," Jenny said softly brushing some hair from her face.

"Hey," she whispered back.

She kissed Janie on the forehead, and reveled for a moment in the love and pure happiness of being a mother.

"I need to apologize to you, sweetie."

Janie tried to focus as she moved her body forward a little.

"You know that you are not a mistake, don't you?" She asked, tears forming in her eyes.

Jenny clasped her heart locket. Out of everything that occurred in her life, Janie was the most precious and right thing that ever happened to her. She was more than her daughter. She helped Jenny become an adult. She learned about patience, kindness, and optimism even in the most horrendous times. Because of Janie, Jacy decided to be a part of their lives. She still did not understand why God took him back home, but she held onto the promise that she would meet him again someday.

Janie glanced at her mother confused.

"I know mom. I was just trying to get my things back from some kids at school. They were only having some fun."

Jenny leaned in to hug her daughter, and Janie willingly accepted it. As Jenny sat back up, Janie grabbed the silver heart around her mother's neck.

"Can I open it?" She pleaded.

Jenny opened the locket to display pictures of Jacy and herself as teenagers.

"I miss daddy," Janie said.

A couple of tears slid down Jenny's cheeks.

"I miss him too, sweetie." To herself she silently added, "Thank you Lord, for this life." She wiped the tears from her face and grabbed Janie's hand to help her off the bed.

"Come on, grandpa has the grill going and he's making hamburgers."

Janie grinned as Jenny led her down the stairs.

"Aw, you know I don't like burgers," she said. "I want a hot dog."

Jenny just laughed as they entered the kitchen.

"Janie!" Shouted Damien and Madilynn running up to her.

Jenny watched with delight while Janie knelt down to give her cousins each a kiss.

"Where's the birthday girl?" Janie asked.

"Here's Lillian, the birthday girl," snickered Kristina handing the tot to Janie.

"Happy birthday, little one," Janie beamed.

"Okay, guys," Marie cut in. "I need a picture with all my grandchildren."

Jim grabbed the camera and Marie stole Lillian from Janie's arms. She knelt to the floor with Janie besides her. Regina put Paul in Janie's arms, while Kristina placed Damien, Madilynn, and Oliver in front of them on the floor.

Jenny stood behind them and prayed. "Thank you Lord for such a wonderful family."

Jenny was proud of her daughter, and excited to see

their family grow larger as each of her siblings had children. She looked at her mother and Marie's face expressed pure happiness with her grandchildren all around her. Jenny's heart swelled with joy. She did not want to rush life, but in the back of her mind, she could not wait to be a grandma too. With Kristina, Jessica, and Regina standing on the other side of the camera, they each shouted and made funny faces to get the little one's attention.

"Say cheese!" Jim said.

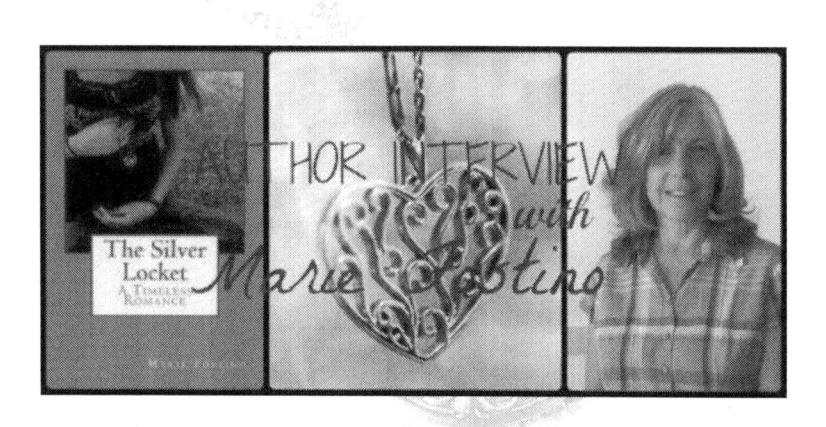

AUTHOR INTERVIEW with Marie Tortino

An edited interview with Marie Fostino and Jessica, from Bottle and Books Reviews Online, on October 31, 2013.

What inspired you to become a writer?

I wrote my first book because of my father in law's Alzheimer's. As I was taking care of him, I would write letters on my computer to family to keep everyone up dated. They told me after he died that I needed to make a book to help others and that is how I started writing. All though I went through a box of letters I found in my garage the other day and noticed that I wrote short stories while my kids were young in the year 1990 and I also have the rejection letters. This was way before computers and cell phones.

What have you written?

I have written 5 books so far. One is non-fiction called Alzheimer's A Caretakers Journal. This was about taking care of my father in law with his Alzheimer's. The other 4 books are fiction YA books.

My book The Silver Locket came to me after my first grandchild turned fifteen years old. The memories came flooding back to that time her mom was pregnant while in high school which was the idea behind this book.

My third book A Struggle of the Heart came next as I looked back into my life when I changed careers from being a beautician to a paramedic due to the Oklahoma City Bombing.

My forth book Rosemary & Antonio is my version of Romeo

and Juliet but in the 1920's. Growing up and living in Chicago, the history of Al Capone is very interesting to me since my grandpa use to work for him.

My fifth book Sometimes Love Hurts is a book about love and forgiveness. Like a lot of marriages we have gone through some rough times and had to learn to forgive and forget.

When writing do you have any rituals (a lucky trinket by your side, mood music, etc.)?

No I don't. I have done a lot of writing of the first draft on my ambulance. I have the idea in my head and just start writing it over and over again until I come up with how I want to present it. I enjoy fiction books so I try to make real life situations into fiction stories.

Are you working on anything at the moment?

I am in the thinking mode right now. All of my books but one is from my life changing experiences.

How long on average does it usually take you to write a book?

This is a hard question. It may not take long to write the book if you have it in your head, but it is the re-editing and re-writing that takes so long.

If you could live in one place, real or fictional, where would it be and why?

I would go back in time and live on the farm in Wisconsin with my grandparents. Life was simple and days were long, whether chasing the chickens to find their eggs or lie back on the grass and make animals out of the clouds, those were the days my friends.

What is your favorite book and why?

The book called The Notebook by Nicholas Sparks holds tight to my heart. I think it is because of my father in law with his Alzheimer's and that is the first book I read that was fiction about the disease.

If you could give your younger self any advice what would it be?

I would have to tell myself to keep a journal of my life. Say starting like right after high school to see how I have grown mentally and spiritually.

How would you describe yourself in five words?

Compassionate, loving, self-motivated, playful, and quiet.

What's next for you as an author?

I am working on getting my other E-books into paper back. I myself enjoy holding a book in my hands. I love reading from my kindle but I miss the smell of a book.

What advice would you give aspiring authors?

If you have a story, write, and re-write. Don't let other people discourage you. Make sure you get your work edited over and over again. Than share it with the world. Remember you can start by making it an E-book which is cheaper than making it a paper back. But who knows, maybe a big time agent will like what you wrote and you can be the next big hit.

Also from the author of

THE SILVER LOCKET

MARIE FOSTINO

Made in the USA
Charleston, SC
30 January 2014